JEANNE'S ROAD

JOCELYNE
SAUCIER

JEANNE'S ROAD

A NOVEL TRANSLATED BY RHONDA MULLINS

Cormorant Books

Canada Council for the Arts Conseil des Arts du Canada

ONTARIO ARTS COUNCIL
CONSEIL DES ARTS DE L'ONTARIO

The publisher gratefully acknowledges the support of the Canada Council for the Arts and the Ontario Arts Council for its publishing program. We acknowledge the financial support of the Government of Canada through the Book Publishing Industry Development Program (BPIDP) for our publishing activities.

We acknowledge the financial support of the Government of Canada, through the National Translation Program for Book Publishing, for our translation activities.

The translator acknowledges the assistance of the Banff International Literary Translation Centre at The Banff Centre in Banff, Alberta, Canada.

Printed and bound in Canada

LIBRARY AND ARCHIVES CANADA CATALOGUING IN PUBLICATION

Saucier, Jocelyne, 1948–
Jeanne's road / Jocelyne Saucier ; Rhonda Mullins, translator.

Translation of: Jeanne sur les routés.
ISBN 978-1-897151-37-2

I. Mullins, Rhonda, 1966– II. Title.
PS8587.A38633J4213 2010 C843 .54 C2009-907173-8

Cover art and design: Angel Guerra/Archetype
Interior text design: Tannice Goddard/Soul Oasis Networking
Printer: Transcontinental

This book is printed on 100% post-consumer waste recycled paper.

CORMORANT BOOKS INC.
215 SPADINA AVENUE, STUDIO 230, TORONTO, ONTARIO, CANADA M5T 2C7
www.cormorantbooks.com

FSC
Recycled
Supporting responsible use of forest resources
Cert no. SW-COC-000952
www.fsc.org
© 1996 Forest Stewardship Council

For Marianne and Lucas

CHAPTER I

IN THE PHOTO, I am seventeen and think I can become someone different one day, although I know it's not to be. I will always struggle with the need to build a better person upon the rubble of myself. On my good days, I tell myself that this need is a need for the absolute, that I am driven by something greater than me, that within me there is an extraordinary drive for accomplishment. But then I hear a mocking voice, shrill in my ear. "So, old girl, still aspiring to sainthood?"

You can see the car and the country road clearly behind the young girl in the photo. It's a faded black-and-white shot, but still you can make out that it's spring. The long, black furrows in the fields, the barren trees, the streaks of a storm brewing or beating its retreat in the sky; the scene is pathetic, sad. Only my father could be moved by it.

He took the picture. He insisted that I keep my rubber boots on and that I hold that stack of newspapers in my arms.

— Smile. You're the hope of the workers.

The year is 1961, in deepest Abitibi, and we are communists. Counter-revolutionaries have just invaded the Bay of Pigs in Cuba, and I find it hard to smile, because I'm inhabited by my father's rage.

— Castro is going to send them packing with a good swift kick in the arse. You'll see.

He had stoked his anger all day. We left at daybreak with a carton full of sandwiches that would have to do for breakfast, lunch, and supper, because we didn't have the money or the time for a restaurant — where would we have found a restaurant in the lost villages where we were delivering the news of a new era?

My feet were cold in my rubber boots, but that wasn't the sort of complaint my father would tolerate. Comfort is a bourgeois concept. We, who lived in exemplary poverty at home, knew this only too well. All those years, my mother, my sisters, and I never shrank from the hardships that the people's fight for the rule of the proletariat required of us.

So I forced a smile, hoping it would satisfy the workers and my father. It was always the same old story. Every time he was about to take my picture, I would ask myself, How should I smile this time? And when I saw the result, I hated the girl with the beatific grin of the blessed. It's hard to believe that I could even muster a smile with his eyes bearing down on me. Even so, I never managed to pull together one that would make me smile.

The photo appeared on the front page of *L'Étincelle* or *L'Étoile* or *L'Aurore*, I don't remember which. My father and I made the rounds delivering so many newspapers. I acquired a taste for the road.

I love watching the pines, the lakes, and the rivers stream by and then, all of a sudden, a sight to behold, golden light creeps over the dark waters of a lake, a small house appears through the morning fog, and then another, and an entire village awakens before me, but I'm already on my way, because there were some villages we avoided. Communists were not welcome everywhere.

— Not to worry. It took the Bolsheviks years to bring the revolution to Russia.

I didn't worry. On the contrary, I was perfectly happy in the car. These are the moments I love to remember. My father, at the wheel of that rattling, coughing old heap, and me, at his side, watching the scenery go by while he made conversation. My father talked, abundantly and passionately, of the Russian Revolution, the Chinese Revolution, the Cuban Revolution, and the revolution underway in America, in spite of McCarthyism, in spite of the Cold War, in spite of anything that could stand in its way. The revolution would overcome.

— And what about Stalin, Dad?

— What about Stalin?

— Stalin, you know, the trials, the executions, the gulags, and all that.

— That's all lies. History will sort out what's what and rehabilitate Stalin's name. You'll see.

I regretted having raised such a touchy subject. There was a long moment of silence, and without my father's voice the road would become dreary and sad.

I'm always on the road. I travel the same cheerless and desolate land, with newspapers filling my car (not communist newspapers — no one's interested in Hegelian dialectics these days anyways), and that full, warm voice that taught me to hope for a better world haunts me still.

— So, young lady, what do you want to talk about?

The voice that I hear in my head is as resonant and perfectly modulated as the one that made conversation in our old clunker of a car. The voice of a man in the prime of his forties.

My father was handsome, like a movie star. He could have been Audrey Hepburn's leading man in *Roman Holiday*, but he settled for the humble life of a militant communist in a country that didn't want to know.

— Didn't want to know? You must be joking! Rouyn was crawling with communists in 1930.

The young girl in the photo stirs deep down inside me. These memories captivate me. I become the young girl of bygone days, listening to her father's voice, waiting for him to tell the tales of his heroic youth.

The adjective is mine. He wouldn't approve of it, heroism being the exclusive domain of the great, while he was just a humble hack. That's how he liked to introduce himself, but I know that he was proud of being a reporter. A pride all the more prideful because he concealed it. This I can relate to, along with tactical humility and working as a reporter. Humility is comfortable when you have learned to practice it in your own private smugness. As for journalism, I was born steeping in it, as they say.

I've been wandering the roads for over thirty years, like my father, with a stack of newspapers in the back seat, and sometimes with two children bundled in blankets, my daughters, who I take with me along the winding roads. I have never felt the pull of domestic life.

—What do you think of a headline like, *A Young Communist Marching toward Victory*?

My father broke his Stalinesque silence to wonder if a triumphant headline was what was called for to caption the photo, or whether he should go for something subtle instead.

— *A Young Communist Working for a Better World*. Would that be better?

He was not really asking for my opinion. He was thinking out loud, and I took notes.

In a large cardboard-bound notebook I noted all the thoughts that popped into his head and that could be published in *L'Étincelle* (or *L'Étoile* or *L'Aurore*, I don't remember anymore). He left me to judge his thoughts. He talked, he carried on a conversation with himself, he presented arguments, he debated before the highest authorities, showed them the flaws in the arguments, put them on trial, pleaded the just cause, went back to his initial premise, and was off again, considering everything that life, the Party, the people, the sky, and everything under it brought to mind … and I sorted through it all.

I worked by transubstantiation, changing one idea into another, emptying the first of its substance, hence, the idea of communist youth embodied by a smile in rubber boots. I just couldn't do the idea justice in the notebook. It raised the hackles of my mind. So I waited for my father to be transported to other thoughts. Spring, for instance. It's bleak, it's melting, it's splattered with washed-out colours, the rose is not yet in bloom, spring has barely sprung, it's grey and gloomy, but it heralds renewal.

— Renewal …

The transubstantiation began.

— *With Spring Comes a New Day for the Workers.*

Spring didn't have any particular resonance in my father's mind. The bloom of the rose, the chirping of the birds, the soft green of the hillsides, he could see them, hear them, feel them, talk about them at great length, but they were just concepts. Spring was just a road through the advance of time. At the end of its fleeting tenderness, the scientific will of history awaited.

— *Springtime Brings with it the Renewal of the Workers' Cause.*

He smiled. He was on the verge of the nirvana of an idea that would satisfy him. I loved this moment when the thought process held us in a tenuous state of intimacy. We could have driven by an elephant on a bicycle, and neither one of us would have commented, so intent were we on capturing the thought that was fluttering around our heads, holding us in suspense. Lord, there were some fine moments on the road with my father.

—*Spring Smiles upon the Workers' Cause.* Yes, that's it, *Spring Smiles upon the Workers' Cause.* It's poetic, and yet militant. Are you getting this down?

I would have preferred that the headline not smile, but I wrote it down anyway. I should have accepted seeing myself on the front page of *L'Étincelle* (or *L'Étoile* or *L'Aurore* ...) under a headline that points to my mouth wide with happiness.

— We'll run the story about Chinese revisionism alongside it.

I want to erase myself completely, erase myself from my memories, but I can't. The smile pops up regularly in the newspapers my father left boxes full of. The newspapers have yellowed, the smile has faded, they have followed me through every change of address, and I still can't manage to be touched by the effort that I made when smiling in the image of a young communist girl.

I prefer, much prefer, the notebooks that record my father's thoughts. I have boxes full of these too. Numbered, categorized, I have taken great care of them. They fill five cardboard boxes that have never been exposed to the humidity of basements or the dust of attics, because the notebooks have always slept with me, under my bed, no matter where my daughters and I laid our heads. My father's voice, when it comes to me in my dreams, recounts entire pages of these notebooks that I have read and reread to the point that I no longer know where my own thoughts fit in.

— Don't forget to send a cheque to the printer.

— Yes Dad.

— And the garage. We have a bill that's a few months old.

Pay printer & mechanic. The notebooks contain more than just tactical and metaphorical considerations on the proletarian revolution. There is the odd stray note that reminds me that we had a day-to-day life in our little apartment on Dallaire Avenue, in what is still called the immigrant quarter.

— The Vinohradoras are moving to Toronto at the end of next week.

The Vinohradoras were our neighbours. Ukrainians. They arrived with the largest wave of immigrants who came from just about everywhere on earth, heeding the call of the Klondike, and now that life was better somewhere else, they were moving on, taking with them my only prospect as a young girl, a boy my own age, Andrew, and his Slavic blue eyes. What would Andrew remember about me? My smile, probably, my greatest asset as a temptress.

— They're having a going-away party.

— At the Ukrainian Hall?

— Of course. Where else?

I always liked social events at the Ukrainian Hall, even the wakes. It was where Andrew and I exchanged our first lovers' glances. I think that we were each as surprised as the other. We grew up together, in a way, our families sharing the same balcony and the same ideas. All the Ukrainians in this town were communists at one time, even if they no longer are.

—The Vinohradoras were great friends of Anna Evaniuk. And Anna Evaniuk, a great friend of Jeanne Corbin.

— It was an incredible time.

And just like that, we are there.

CHAPTER 2

THE YOUNG GIRL in the photo spent a long time believing in the divine nature of a love that cannot be. She let the beautiful Andrew fly off to Toronto without a promise to write, without even asking for a picture of him, preferring instead to spend years romanticizing and crying over love lost. Our lives are what they are, and mine has been spent dreaming dreams that are larger than life, larger than love.

I have memories that can't be shared. This town, for example, that has no particular identity and is the backdrop to my father's tales. Rouyn is a misleading town, a mining town without miners. There are no more men dragging their feet along the sidewalk to the siren's call of the shift change. The mine shut down ages ago, but the town still calls itself the national copper capital because of the smelting works and sulphuric acid plant that replaced the black pit of the mine and that give the place an air of a lunar Las Vegas. At night, when the Noranda Mines facilities are lit up, you'd think a transatlantic liner had sunk into intergalactic oblivion.

I was born and grew up in this town, but I don't relate to it at all. Small northern towns are idiosyncratic in that they believe only in the future of now, and I, who believed in a slow and inevitable advance of thought that would propel humanity into an eternal and egalitarian state of happiness, hold no affection for the glass facades and pink granite, pretty though they may be, that spread throughout my town.

Is there anyone left who remembers that there was a small society of nations here that lived on Moscow time?

— We even had a returnee from Moscow!

A "returnee from Moscow," in the coded language of my father and his comrades, was the lucky person chosen by the Party to make a reconnaissance trip to the fatherland of the workers.

My father never made the pilgrimage into Soviet territory; he was never a member of the Party or any of its organizations, and he firmly but tenderly refused to give the reason for this anytime I tried to broach the subject. There's nothing in my notebooks to enlighten me on the matter.

— Lujanen made the trip.

Lujanen was a hero of the Clérion strike. He was with Raketti, Baillargeon, and Huart when they roused the lumberjacks' ire in the fall of 1933 and led them into a futile strike. Like Raketti, who was also of Finnish descent, but American by birth, he was imprisoned and deported.

Lujanen, Ahlquist, Hnatyshyn: these giants were my father's heroes, and they would find their way into the conversation at the drop of a hat. While I was writing down the names racing by, names with double, triple, and quadruple consonants that cramped my fingers, I waited for the sweet name of Jeanne Corbin, my childhood heroine, to appear amid the glory of these tales.

I have never seen her, never met her, and yet I know her well. I know that she smiled without really smiling, that her features lit up at any of life's little pleasures, and that when confronted with difficulty or strife, nothing moved under the fine skin of her face. She didn't suffer from mood swings, from irritable bilious discharge or muted and tormented rumblings. Jeanne got angry only when she had to, and then she exploded into a clear stream of words.

I know her as intimately as I know myself. She has occupied my thoughts ever since I was old enough to remember.

She is twenty-seven years old. Eternally. Whether she appears in my girlhood memories or my aging woman's thoughts, Jeanne is always twenty-seven, and she reminds me of the goodness of life. She was an optimist, Jeanne; she was undaunted in the face of difficulty. She believed in decent pay for labour, victory in adversity, the progress of humanity, and, with her clear gaze, she could convince anyone of the purity of her intentions.

— Brown, she had brown eyes.

— What?

— Her eyes. They were brown. Velvety brown.

Her velvety eyes hidden behind large dark glasses and a cloche hat.

—The hat was to foil the police photographers.

Jeanne Corbin was a militant from the word *go*. She was only twenty-seven when she gave her famous speech before the giant-size portrait of Lenin at the Ukrainian Labour Temple, but she had a long past of clandestine meetings, samizdat newspapers, messages in code, furtive moves to slip police raids and searches. The Communist Party of Canada was declared illegal in 1931. Tim Buck, Tom McEwen, and John Boychuck, its main leaders, were in prison. Jeanne had files with the RCMP and Comintern. Her movements were tracked and her writings dissected; only her private thoughts belonged to her alone.

She appeared in my life before I was born. My father was a young newlywed, my mother was pregnant with my older sister, and I was not yet of this world and certainly not at the Ukrainian Labour Temple when she made her famous speech. And yet I still can recite large parts of it today. *For every comrade arrested, ten more will stand and take up the torch in the fight*, and *We will oppose the servants of imperialism with a picket line that is as hard as rock*, and *If there are not enough men on the picket lines, the women will join them*.

Over the years in our room in the tiny two-bedroom apartment where we lived above a general store, my sisters and I made our own fun with a play that recreated that speech:

me, in front of the pint-sized poster of Lenin, addressing a crowd of angry lumberjacks — played by my sister Clara, who punctuated my tirades with a hearty "United on the picket line" — and at the end of the room, my other sister, frustrated because she had the bad role, stalking back and forth and sending furious glances our way. Alexandra was playing Sergeant Turnbull, the enemy of the people, who would charge Jeanne with sedition and incitement to riot. We made him as ugly as possible: broom-like eyebrows drawn in with grey crayon, a steel-wool beard, and a pillow pot belly. In truth, he was a young man of thirty-one, muscular and determined, with an incredibly focused gaze, a Mona Lisa smile, and not a wisp of grey. I've seen the pictures.

Alexandra did not tolerate being booed by an assembly of lumberjacks for very long, and our Ukrainian Labour Temple meeting ended in a quarrel long before Jeanne could finish her speech. Our mother had to step in to put an end to the squabbling.

Nobody wanted to play Turnbull, and nobody fought for the role of Jeanne, because it was understood that I would make the speech; it was the four hundred lumberjacks in the room who were at the centre of the dispute. If discussions were heated enough before the performance, no matter who ended up personifying lumberjack pride, Clara and Alexandra would have spewed their venom, and Jeanne could, without worrying about an angry outburst from Turnbull, conclude her speech with *solidarity will win this strike*.

We knew the speech by heart, down to the last comma; we had learned it at a tender age at our father's knee. Evenings, when we wouldn't go to sleep, he would take us in his arms and rock us while reciting the long monotone chant and its crusading moments, but with a voice so tender that we would slip off to the land of dreams, taking with us images of a deep tranquility. I remember fighting off sleep to hear my father's voice go on.

We share this memory, my sisters and I. Our father bent over our sleep, his long hands gathering the flannelette of our nightgowns around our childish bodies, murmuring a lullaby that heralded the victory of the workers, set to music as soft as tissue paper. Nearby, our mother set about the quiet tasks of the early evening, sacred music sung in unison with our father. And then the image would softly materialize. A woman as beautiful as a dream would rise up against the enemy, slinging words that had the mortifying purity of diamonds.

Was Jeanne Corbin pretty? It's important that a heroine, even a communist one, be pretty. But never having met her, never having seen her, I had no way of knowing, and Jeanne remained faceless throughout those years. My sisters were luckier. They had met Jeanne Corbin.

Clara and Alexandra are older than me by some ten years. For all intents and purposes, they are the same age because only eleven months separate them. If it hadn't been for Clara's blond hair and Alexandra's dark, thick locks, they could have easily passed for twins. They were born in the same breath, and they used the same mocking voice to chant "grown-up Jeanne has beauty and grace, little Jeanne has a potty face."

I was five years old, six when political theatre consumed our free time in our bedroom. Our room was barely large enough for a bed pushed up against the wall to save space, with a photo of Lenin pinned up above it. On either side of the bed were chairs where our clothes were laid out for the next day, and opposite these, against the other wall, a chest of drawers with ample space for our wardrobes, while next to it, a closet held the rest.

I made my speech standing on the big bed, with Lenin looking on protectively. An old hat of my mother's was the only thing I had to disguise me as the passionate militant. A veiled hat. The existence of the cloche hat was revealed to me only years later.

I clearly remember the questions that nagged at the little five-year-old girl in the bedroom as she shouted herself hoarse to stir up the passions of the lumberjacks. Am I pretty enough? Pretty enough to deserve to don Jeanne's image? Is my nose too round? Are my teeth too gapped, too square, not thin enough?

I hadn't yet developed my obsession with smiles, but I think that it can be traced back to that little girl asking herself whether she was too, or not enough, whether she was worthy of the performance, whether Jeanne was watching her from the great beyond, whether her revered communist hand would bless her, whether, whether. Little girls of the world, don't ever let others study you from afar!

Jeanne's faceless gaze and my father's voice have been with me for so long that if one of them were to disappear, I think I would disappear with it. All that would remain of me would be a long trail of dust somewhere along the road. A dog would bark. He would see a grey Sunbird pass by, and then nothing, the Sunbird would take flight, because its sole occupant had no one left to talk to in her head.

Jeanne doesn't speak, she doesn't answer my calls. She just hails me with a benevolent look and then softly fades, while my father's voice is very real. I would like to hold on to Jeanne's spirit. I would like her gaze to light up her face and reveal to me her eyes, her forehead, and her mouth.

—Was she pretty?

— She was French.

—And?

— French women are pretty without being pretty.

I knew I shouldn't ask the question. Does one expect Rosa Luxemburg to be pretty? And Marx, who changed the face of the world, do we need to know whether or not he was handsome? And Mao, and Stalin, no, forget Stalin, and Castro, did they need movie-star good looks to lead their people to revolution?

I was treated to one of his rants of indignation that circled the planet, gathering in its swell the imperialist disgraces of trust holders and national bourgeoisies, the just anger of the oppressed, Vietnam's NLF, Angola's MPLA, they were all in there, and at the heart of this inferno, I wrote, *She was pretty without being pretty*.

So she is to be imagined as elegant, skilled at using artifice to make her look her best, an intelligent beauty who knows how to smile and move and who metes out her quiet charm in small doses.

—That's not it at all. Jeanne was not uptown elegant. She was a militant, heart and soul.

I knew that Jeanne was not an uptown piece of fluff, but it was good to shake him up a little. He was very forthcoming when it came to convincing me of the magnificent era he had lived through, the Clérion strike, the Fros strike — *Fros* was the word we used for foreigners — the feeling that took hold in the streets of Rouyn that a new world was looming, the feeling of having been touched by the sword of grace when he heard Jeanne speak at the Ukrainian Labour Temple, her trial, prison. He had told me everything he knew about her, her birth in Cellettes, her childhood in Tofield, but I had never met her. I wanted to be able to imagine her eyes, her lips, her mouth: I wanted to draw a face for her. Was she pretty underneath her cloche hat?

— She had a beauty spot here.

And with a single finger, daunted by where it was going to rest, he showed me an imaginary spot under the right earlobe.

CHAPTER 3

JEANNE CORBIN ENTERED our lives December 9, 1933. She arrived from Timmins, a mining town in Northern Ontario where the Central Committee had assigned her one year before. She had not fallen out of favour; on the contrary, the Fourth District of the Party, which included Abitibi and Nouvel-Ontario, was one of the most active communist cells in the country. She was the district secretary of the Canadian Labour Defence League and was responsible for the French-language communist press. Her travels had exhausted her; they kept her on the road between Toronto, Montreal, and the many hot spots in the district, because this was during the cruellest days of the Great Depression, and revolt was brewing. Lumberjacks in Kapuskasing, Hearst, and Spruce Falls were on strike, and Jeanne was raising money, hiring lawyers, haranguing crowds, and writing furiously, for *La Vie ouvrière* and for *The Worker*, translating from one to the other, overseeing their distribution, their financing, and ensuring they remained clandestine. She was completely worn out on the evening of December 9th.

My sisters and I never considered Jeanne's state of exhaustion. We imagined her fresh as a daisy, taking to the Ukrainian Labour Temple podium with a light step and delivering the famous speech in a single breath. How could we have imagined otherwise? The main character in our bedroom theatre couldn't possibly have had any weaknesses.

My father was there on December 9, 1933. As a reporter, he was able to move about the room at will, track the scent of lumberjack wherever it led, and follow Turnbull, who was advancing stealthily through the crowd. He was captivated by the words, frozen in front of the podium except for the pencil flying across his notebook. The words carried him into an unfamiliar universe. *The time has come when workers will sing the glorious song of justice*, the young woman on the podium said.

He was twenty-eight, vaguely anxious, with beliefs that unravelled at every turn, but he was certain that life would take him where it should. He had followed the road of the jobless. North Bay, Sudbury, Kirkland Lake: his point of departure was Belle River, his birthplace, where he had left a young wife while he hunted down work that would provide for them: him, his wife, and the recently announced baby. Toronto, Oshawa, North Bay, and finally Rouyn. The road to freedom. Men of any nationality could find work: Finns, Croats, Byelorussians, and Lord knows who else, immigrants, the unemployed, misfits of all sorts chased from the anaemic cities of the south, their only hope and passage hands that said they were accustomed to heavy loads and labour humbly accepted.

My father had fine, nervous hands, long hands that fluttered like curtains in the wind and settled softly when the shiver of speaking subsided. They were not hands that could turn up at the site office of a mine.

He had been told as much while on the road. You won't find work with those hands. And he was shown large, twisted hands, some missing a digit or two.

Yet those were the hands that landed him a job at the *Rouyn-Noranda Press*. His long hands that were flipping through *Le Devoir* in a tumbledown shack serving spaghetti. At the next table, a man was watching his hands flit from one page to the next, impressed by their familiarity with the paper, their lightness, their dexterity, and, most importantly, their contentment when, after coming together to close one page, they opened to a new world to contemplate. If that young man speaks decent English, the man said to himself, I'll hire him.

And so life was good once again for my father. D.A. Jones was the editor of the *Rouyn-Noranda Press*, and my father, who was Franco-Ontarian and therefore perfectly bilingual, answered in English with no trace of an accent when Jones asked him if the spaghetti was to his liking.

Our life in this place started the moment that my father entered into that conversation with D.A. Jones about unappetizing spaghetti, which he described as fortifying, civil obsequiousness that the abominable Jones responded to in kind, blahblahblah and blahblahblah. My mother arrived a few weeks later with our meagre household effects.

It's no surprise that we sympathized with the immigrants; we shared the same lives. But who would have thought that we would become redder than the reddest Ukrainians in town?

My father, when he began that conversation with D.A. Jones, who was not yet the abominable Jones, because the Clérion strike had not yet started and he had not yet written an editorial about it, my father was just one of the many young men mobilized by the rumour of work somewhere down the road. And his opening *Le Devoir* was not out of some intellectual affectation on his part, good lord, no! The only form of vanity my father suffered from was that he had none. He was just happy to be able to open the pages of a newspaper that spoke his language. In Belle River, French was a shameful language.

It was not intellectualism that drove him to communism, but a frail young woman who lifted up the crowd with her words, the power of which he could not yet fathom.

Jeanne Corbin addressed the lumberjacks in French at the Ukrainian Labour Temple, and we were all under the spell of the language that she spoke with conviction and elegance. Our bedroom theatre was a very modest re-enactment of a great moment.

Sometimes my mother was in the audience for our afternoon performances, and when the part came when Jeanne talked about her childhood in Tofield, she would clasp her hands, sit back in her chair, and close her eyes. It was her favourite passage. Jeanne talked about how in a godforsaken part of northern Alberta her parents wore themselves to the bone over miserly land, good only for oil. She had learned the value of work, hope through sowing, the daily effort of renewing one's hope for the next day, the irreconcilable need to see one's efforts rewarded one season to the next, and then poof, new times would open up.

— New times ...

My mother smiled.

Jeanne had that grace.

The image of the French peasant couple pried open some room for emotion in the crowd. They were all half-peasants, the lumberjacks who were still dumbfounded by the daring of their strike, hicks as they say, men who had stumped, worked, sowed among the fell, and who became lumberjacks between summers to ward off starvation. And they saw in the French peasants the image of their own despair bent over the hope of their labour.

Jeanne had experience with crowds. From her first communist speech, before children that time, the Young Pioneers of the Ukrainian Labour Temple in Edmonton, the Party had taken her under its austere wing. That was in 1925, when Jeanne was eighteen years old. She was in Edmonton to finish her studies because the little school in Tofield was no longer enough, and she became a communist novice by contagion:

everyone was a communist at the boarding house where she lived. Her speech to the Young Pioneers earned her a police file and, in turn, cost her the teaching job she was destined for. It also saw her taken in hand by the Party. From that point on, her life fused with that of the Party. She found friendship there, the safety of doctrine, the study of sacred texts — Marx, Lenin, and later Ryerson, the only true great intellectual Canadian communism ever produced — and the heady feeling of militant activity that would make her forget everything about herself, the stirrings of her soul, the cries from her heart, the fragility of her health, even her shyness when she had to address a crowd.

— But what eloquence!

My father, who was right near the podium, was also susceptible to the beauty of the image of the French couple bent over the promise of their labour.

Jerry Donohue and Anna Evaniuk had preceded her at the podium. Jerry Donohue was a union organizer, and Anna Evaniuk was the local representative of the Canadian Labour Defence League. I still have their speeches in my boxes. My father's sprawling writing runs over pages and pages of a large black spiral notebook tracking their speeches, but when Jeanne's turn came to address the lumberjacks, only one incomplete sentence appears.

My friends, she began, according to the black notebook, *do not let yourself be intimidated by a few uniforms, because I am going to tell you a fact* ... and the sprawling, generous writing peters out to a snake of a line. My father was transported above the words and recorded nothing more in his notebook.

— Her voice. She had a deep, throaty voice.

He was transported by Jeanne's voice and let the words be etched into him, one by one, cascading, in long tirades, in curtains of sound, without forgetting a single pause, a single lift in her voice. We drew indescribable joy from this indelible memory of my father's, because the speech united us in like-minded adoration.

My father was there, at the Ukrainian Labour Temple, captivated by Jeanne's words, so much so that he no longer had to transcribe them. The words imprinted themselves on his soul as they left the podium and scattered about the room.

Because I'm going to tell you a fact, that the laws of the country are like elastic.

Jeanne was trying to reassure the crowd. That very morning, Raketti, one of the strike leaders, had been arrested. It was Sergeant Turnbull's first blow since the beginning of the labour unrest.

My sister Alexandra, eyebrows askew and a pillow potbelly that came up to her armpits, paced the room imitating the measured step of a wolf tracking its prey in a hostile environment.

Turnbull felt the mood of the crowd shift. The lumberjacks' anger had tarried until now. One by one the men had laid down their axes and their handsaws, from one logging camp to the next, and they had walked through the deep snow — we had never seen such a snowy November — and with heavy feet they went to convince their comrades at the next camp to do the same, ten miles, thirty miles, fifty miles more in the snow, until eight hundred of them had deserted the logging camps. The wrath of the forest giants ran deep indeed.

And the whole time behind the troop of giants, a few policemen walked through the snow at the same pace.

It had been that way since they started out. Tens, hundreds of lumberjacks walking in the footsteps of their anger, through the forest, along town roads, with two or three policemen behind them, no more — Staff Sergeant Kenneth H. Turnbull who was in command of the provincial police detachment in Rouyn had a dozen men at the most.

And then, the picket line was hardening by the hour.

Turnbull felt in the young woman's words that a fury greater than despair would whip up the lumberjacks' simmering anger. Jeanne reminded them that the company had turned its back on them, that it had refused their most meagre demands. She repeated over and over that they were within their rights, that they had nothing to fear from the uniformed puppets who were raising the spectre of their puppet laws.

The laws are just papier mâché created by a bourgeoisie that doesn't know what it is to work with the sweat of their brow from sun-up to sundown.

This is where the image of the French couple intervened.

The image sent a shiver through the assembly of giants, my mother smiled to the gods that protected her, and I bellowed, as loud as my five years would allow, *Gone are the times when workers must bleed themselves dry to put food on the tables of the rich. New times are upon us.*

— Her voice caught in her throat. There was a moment when I was afraid she would collapse on the podium.

It sometimes saddened my father to think that Jeanne was not made for this life. Such a meagre constitution for such a great destiny. And then he would immediately regret such a morose thought.

My voice did not catch in my throat, but I paused, waiting for Jeanne to catch her breath, and then continued.

It was during this pause that my sister Alexandra — no longer able to stand the potbellied, bearded role foisted upon her — got rid of the pillow, the steel wool, and the thick eyebrows and hurried off to the closet to get into another character. I hadn't yet launched into Jeanne's sermon about the picket line when Alexandra reappeared in a grey overcoat and a fedora, pencil and notebook in hand, and came forward in a long, slow movement, beaming as she advanced toward the discovery of a doctrine that would transform our lives.

We will oppose the servants of imperialism with a picket line that is as hard as rock.

Jeanne set out to show the need for solidarity on the picket line. My sister Clara supported her fervently, "United on the picket line," and my mother, absorbed by the idea of the rewards of a new world, repeated each word in hushed tones.

If there are not enough men on the picket lines, the women will join them.

We knew the scene, but every time we felt the same emotion. Alexandra would reach the foot of the bed. We would wait for Jeanne's final words. And while everything was falling into place for the end of the speech, I would feel the devotion in the room shift toward Alexandra. They would no longer be looking at me, listening to me. I would no longer hold anyone's attention, I could barely hear myself, so concentrated was I on what was to come.

Finally, the moment we'd been waiting for since the beginning would be upon us, the last scene, that moment of grace when I uttered Jeanne's final words and when Alexandra would lift her hands to the heavens and collapse in our father's old overcoat.

Solidarity will win this strike.

— Her smile ... her smile at the end of the speech! Pure joy filled with an indefinable sadness. Her entire focus on the advance of the world was in that smile.

My father fell in love and became a communist in one fell swoop.

CHAPTER 4

I feel as though I was born knowing the whole story. My father loved a woman other than my mother, and that love, far from visiting tragedy upon our family, was the thing that cemented it, because Jeanne was the centre of gravity for our most exciting moments. Jeanne on the road, Jeanne before the crowd, Jeanne in prison, Jeanne who went wherever the winds of revolt were blowing, with her small boiled-cardboard suitcase and her smile that was not quite a smile: the story was ours to dream about from our earliest childhood. My sisters and I would tell it to ourselves until we felt it throbbing with life. It was our fairy tale, our Arabian Nights, an incredible fable that kept the three of us warm in the hollow of our shared bed. One would start to tell it, the other holding some of the less threadbare parts in reserve, and I would always ask for more. What did she say to him? What did she say to him after her court appearance? And during their first tryst, what did she say to him? I knew the answers. What mattered was staying in the eye of the story.

We met her when she was very young, making the crossing with her parents that would bring them to America. From the trip she kept only the memory of the odours and the image of the snow upon their arrival. A thousand people crammed into second class for twelve days, our father explained, gives off a strong animal odour. North American second class, he told us, is like European third class. What I retained from all this was the Christmas card image that had dazzled young Jeanne. They docked in the middle of a snowstorm in the port of Saint John, New Brunswick. A snowstorm on April 12th! My sister Alexandra, who never knew how to edit her thoughts, made the unfortunate remark, "The French people's blood must have turned to sausage." My father was not amused.

There were so many ways to be moved by this young girl lost in the solitude of the Alberta plains between two parents who were slaves to the duties of tending a miserly land, and then, suddenly, as a teenager, the wonder of the city, Edmonton, a host of friendships, beautiful, generous, endless discussions, the discovery of an international fraternity, all those young people, like her, immigrants or sons and daughters of immigrants, who were fighting for the liberation of the people: the Young Communists.

What particularly touched me, and what still moves me today, is the long journey along the roads of Canada.

I never get tired of imagining a little slip of a woman, not even five feet tall, probably already weakened by illness, embarking upon the relentlessness of the road. She was not an adventurer, not a nomad; she was the daughter of farmers, bound by the demands of duty, and she was not afraid of anything, not even of failing in the mission she had been given. Grace dwelled within Jeanne.

For a long time now, I have stayed on the road out of the simple desire to roam. I no longer have a mission, no longer have life-saving faith; I have misplaced the meaning of life. Roaming like this for the pure pleasure of it is pathetic when I have Jeanne in my life holding up the canopy of heaven with her hope. On the road Jeanne fears nothing, because she has a mission.

That Jeanne was twenty-four years old. She had left Edmonton a few years before, called by the Central Committee in Toronto, and she was a communist through and through: she did not doubt. Lenin, Marx, and, above all, Stalin, who reigned supreme at the time, watched over her spirit.

She was sent on a subscription drive for *The Worker*, a thankless job. After all, who had a quarter for a communist newspaper in such hard times? But Jeanne had the soul of a militant, and she saw difficulties as mountains to scale on the way to the great valley of the joy of the people. So she took the train, waited for the bus, travelled in a comrade's pickup, slept on the sofa in a comrade's living room or with the children, wolfed down a sandwich, and was off again. Montreal, Ottawa, Winnipeg, Regina: she hit the big cities along the Trans-Canada but turned off when there was a settlement of workers to the north or the south. At Port Arthur, she met the communist troops of the district. In Moose Jaw, Dunlane, and Dinsmore, she made the rounds of the picnics. It was summer and comrades, particularly Ukrainian and Finnish comrades, would get together in parks or on the forest's edge for great picnics with dancing and singing from the old country, and Jeanne, standing on a soapbox like a preacher in an American movie, would address the crowd.

Were they touched by her grace? Did her words penetrate their souls?

— Four hundred six dollars and eighteen cents: that's all she raised in four months. The Party barely covered her costs.

But faith has wings, my father said, and it would take more than mere material considerations to keep our Jeanne down.

— She knew that hands that toiled were hands that hoped.

Hands that toil, hands that hope. The expression became as familiar as sunshine after rain. We would use it at the drop of a hat. Hands that toil, hands that hope, hope is within reach, hope is for one and all, hope belongs to those who want it, and a little butter with that this morning? No problem, hands that toil, hands that hope! The expression is Ukrainian, Croatian, Polish, or Czech. I never knew exactly. It came from the immigrant workers Jeanne met along the Trans-Canada, and it was one of our family treasures.

My sister Clara claimed that the expression came from Finland, that it was what the men and women who sang of their country used to say. *Hands that toil, hands that hope*, they would say, and their large rough hands would drop a coin in Jeanne's hat.

I let Clara claim what she wanted. While my sisters had the chance to meet Jeanne, to see the slow smile spread across her face, to hear the voice that gave the famous speech, they didn't have all those years with my father. They had left home by the time he took me on the road with him; they didn't have access to his thoughts, and, from the notebooks that recorded my father's innermost recesses, I know that hope isn't a vague, poetic notion. Hope is harsh and difficult, it's a daily struggle. It's all we have when we have nothing.

Everywhere along the road, Jeanne met men whose eyes were misty with nostalgia, who would tell her in a faltering English that hands that toil are hands that hope. Spreading their large gnarled hands before her, they would tell her of the work those hands had done, explain their scars, bruises, and missing fingers, brandish their hands proudly, predict a bright future for them in the blast furnace, the mines, or the forest. Work is all I have, they would tell her, folding their hands again.

All that it would take was for the expression to slip out of our father's tales for it to start to resonate in all sorts of ways. We grabbed hold of it like the most precious thing in the world, and we let it roam at will in our lives. It comes up often in my notebooks, next to thoughts that most of the time concern immigrant workers.

I remember once I wanted to make our pet saying part of Jeanne's speech. I very quickly realized the folly of my idea. I was at the part where, after having raised the image of Jeanne's parents, the French farmers wearing themselves to the bone over their land of clay, I was getting ready to launch into the most beautiful part of the speech, the exhortation to strikers to join the picket line.

It seemed to me that the French couple knew that hands that toiled were hands that hoped, that the image was perfectly suited to them, and I uttered the revered words among the others. What an incredible commotion! What wicked heresy! Little girls of the world, curb your spontaneity!

That time, Alexandra was playing the crowd of lumberjacks, and the role of the paunchy Turnbull had fallen to Clara. Our mother was there, sitting on her little chair, eyes closed, hands clasped. She was smiling at the two farmers who were sending her greetings from their fields in far-off Alberta. "A lovely couple," she told me one day, "a couple united in adversity."

And the words hit. *Hands that toil, hands that hope*, I said with all the resonance of my five years, without a thought for the fact that adding a line to the sacred speech was unspeakable heresy.

I have never witnessed anything so surreal. My sisters and my mother, all three mouths gaping, were snatching at the air like nurslings interrupted, and I, courageous little militant that I was, had my arm raised, voice poised to drive the crowds to the barricades, but the words wouldn't come, and in one voice united they resumed Jeanne's speech where I had left it and sang the chorus of that magnificent line, *Gone are the times when workers must bleed themselves dry to put food on the tables of the rich. New times are upon us.*

My voice joined theirs and the performance continued in complete surreality, the four of us, like the chorus of a Greek tragedy, reciting Jeanne's crusading speech in long, slow bursts of sound, until, at the end, Clara fell into a swoon in our father's overcoat.

— I did not fall into a swoon.

CHAPTER 5

— I DID NOT fall into a swoon.

He didn't like our idea of having him collapse in front of the podium at the Ukrainian Labour Temple. He didn't like it, but he was willing to talk about it. Any excuse to take us back to that time.

We were in the wide-open flat spaces of the desolation that is Abitibi. The fields had been cleared, cultivated, abandoned, and all that was left was fallow land with the forest looking on in the distance. The route unwound, sovereign and straight through the sea of grass, and I waited for tales of glorious times. Because they were coming. As surely as the earth is flat in Abitibi, and my father and I were alone in a car delivering the good news, I knew that I was going to hear tales of a heroic era. An era of marches, massive demonstrations, a thousand people gathered in front of the Finn Hall for May 1st, imagine! A thousand people proclaiming the glory of communism, when six years before, all that had stood here was a section of forest frequented by a few prospectors with a vision. Imagine!

I listened to stories told a thousand times and waited for the next episode, which would never come. My father wouldn't tell the story of the night after Jeanne's speech.

Instead, I would hear about this town over and over, and it was an oddball sort of place. A floating island, Noah's ark adrift in the forest. You can't imagine what Rouyn was like until you've heard it told by my father.

— We felt like we were at the centre of the ends of the earth, at the beginning of our lives, that we could do whatever we wanted to anything we chose.

The town was a real mixed bag. Cabins, hastily built roads, stores, restaurants, clapboard structures, log structures, and then next thing you know, chickens and cows, a farm next door to a bank, and not much farther along, next to the public baths, a Lebanese-owned opium den, and not much farther still, because all of this was squeezed side by side against the encroaching forest and the lake, Lake Osisko, a magnificent lake that served as a dumping ground for poisonous waste from the mine that was enthroned on the other shore and at the foot of which there was another small town, Noranda, a very quiet town that belonged to the mining company. And I haven't mentioned the blind pigs, the brothels, and the churches. Because the town had everything, the good and the bad, merrily rubbing shoulders: there was something for everyone.

It's no surprise that the immigrant workers laid down their belongings in Rouyn. At the end of the road they had travelled, there was a new Eldorado, and the northern air filling their lungs, the smell of pine carried on a slightly bitter wind, reminding them of the land they had left back in the Ukraine, Poland, or Croatia. And they settled in as if they were still back home, with their icons, their songs, their nostalgia, and their gnarled hands. They built a place where they could be free men.

The town had places where you could dance the mazurka just like in Warsaw, drink slivovitz with friends, share the new joke about the little shepherd boy from the Carpathians, or cry over a lost love in the arms of a cousin. There were places for Croatian Christmas, Polish Christmas, Russian Christmas, Ukrainian Christmas, Finnish Christmas: every nationality the least bit represented threw up a building where its people could sing, dance, eat, and drink like they did in the old country. Why did the Finns and the Ukrainians baptize theirs with such grandiose names? Because most of them had arrived from the western provinces where they were lumberjacks, farmers, and communists, where they had a Ukrainian Labour Temple and a Finnish Labour Temple sponsored by the Communist Party, and they had found warmth, comfort, and hope there. The Great Depression had thrown them out into the streets, and they had rebuilt their temple of hope here.

They used to sing and dance at the labour temples, too. As my father used to say, put two Ukrainians together and they'll form a mandolin trio.

The labour temple was where the birthdays of Lenin and Stalin, the anniversaries of the Paris Commune and the Russian Revolution were celebrated, and it was the site of the unforgettable demonstration of May 1, 1932. A thousand people in front of the Finn Hall, a thousand people, out of a population that barely numbered five thousand. Just imagine!

My father would stick to the valiant deeds of this heroic era. He wouldn't tell me about the night after Jeanne's speech at the Ukrainian Labour Temple. I suspect he had no memory of it. His mind would become muddled when trying to recall the elusive hours of that night.

As towns go, Rouyn wasn't big enough to get lost in, and yet that night he went down into the cold, snowy streets, walking until he was no longer aware of what his feet were doing, and he was lost in the night. He took a road until it led him to the black night of the forest, and then he turned his steps toward the flickering lights of the town and continued his phantom walk to the end of the main street, where Jos Dallaire kept his cows, to the end of Perreault Street, to the Noranda Mines shaft, to the miners' barracks, the mine manager's house, and then again to the Dallaire farm, to the raw silhouette of the mine ... he went round and round in circles, his feet in step with his reeling thoughts. He arrived home in the wee hours, without his hat, his overcoat flapping open, and a glint of madness in his eyes. My mother was the one who told me about it.

"I knew right away that something had happened to him."

She had waited the whole time, thinking he had strayed into one of the town's many blind pigs, which was unlike him, and when she opened the door to him, she knew he had returned from a very long journey. Gently, as one would with someone who is seriously ill, she took his coat, dried his hair, and sat him at the kitchen table with a steaming ginger toddy in his hands.

She was prepared to hear just about anything, but not the frenzied tale that she couldn't begin to comprehend and that she had to hear again from the beginning in order to understand that at the centre of this muddle stood a woman alone on a podium, fanning the flame of a new line of thought that had captured her husband's soul. She didn't have so much as a shadow of an impulse of panic.

"A saint. She was a saint."

My mother was not the woman we knew from our childhood who was game for any form of worship. She was young then, barely twenty-five, pregnant up to her armpits — she would give birth to my sister Alexandra two months later. She was a woman who was viscerally part of the chain of life and yet already marked by a mystical quest that would have her running to every religious service going in town. She recognized a kindred spirit in the woman getting worked up on the podium.

"A saint. She was a saint. There is nothing to fear from a saint."

That night, standing in front of the kitchen table, my father recited the speech in a haunted voice, while she listened devotedly and patiently, and when, at the end, he was overcome by the passion of the final line and collapsed into a chair, she asked quite simply whether the woman on the podium was wearing a hat.

And that's when Jeanne's hat made its first appearance in our story.

It's strange that a woman so lacking in vanity could have moved an entire family with a simple piece of felt. When I was preparing to get up on the bed and my sisters noticed that my head was bare, they scrambled to jam my mother's old veiled hat on my head. "You're not thinking of giving Jeanne's speech without a hat!"

—I don't know why your mother got stuck on that detail. Hat, no hat, what's the difference?

"I wanted to know whether a personal detail had registered with him."

That was our mother through and through: a little mouse, secretly gnawing away, trying to tear off her morsel of happiness. She would not have tackled head-on the problem presented by this orator, alone in front of a crowd of men, possibly beautiful and seductive. She had to know whether he had been moved in intimate terms, by legs prettily displayed with the swing of a dress, by the elegance of a gesture, by a little something and nothing that would make its mark on his flesh. The hat was what seemed to her the most innocuous, the least compromising.

My mother was impervious to any kind of sorrow. She was a happy soul. She sang simple airs to herself that she heard on the radio, changing the words to suit her fancy. I still remember a little ditty about the burst of colour of a tablecloth in the sunlight, a knob of butter melting on mashed potatoes, the fragrance of freshly washed sheets, and zip-a-dee-doo-dah, how wonderful life is with a loving man at the table, how nice it is to serve him hot soup, and how we must praise God on High for having put happiness in our path.

I believe she made a pact with herself when she discovered how much room a woman was taking up in her husband's soul. She resolved that he would not be alone there, that we would all follow that road, she and the children she would give birth to. We would all love Jeanne with one united love.

Did she design her mystical quest for happiness in the disorder of that night, or was it her nature never to turn from the light, never to hear anything but that internal music that she spread about her? My sisters, whose memories go back farther, tell me that she was always that way, joyous and light, and that her religiosities started well before my birth.

"Religiosities" is a word that must be used in the plural in this case, because her devotions went in every direction. She went to every church in town, except the synagogue on Ninth Street. If the Jews had been more sociable, she undoubtedly would have ended up studying the Torah, so exuberant was her faith. But they formed a closed ghetto at the time, like the Chinese, mind you, whom we never saw outside of their restaurants. Where did the Chinese worship? My mother herself couldn't have said.

I have this image of my mother, young and pretty, bursting in to the apartment and saying, "What a sermon, children. What beautiful words of solace!" She would sit down in the first chair she saw because her Sunday shoes pinched, and while she rubbed her throbbing feet, she would tell us about the priest's entrance, the clouds of incense, the smoke from the candles, the hymns sung at the top of the congregation's lungs, and the sermon that she interpreted however she liked because she didn't understand a word of Slovenian or Polish, or any of the missionary priests who made the rounds of flocks lost in the Canadian expanse and who officiated in the basement of the Blessed Sacrament Church. The Russian Orthodox mass was agony, because it was three long hours without a moment to sit (even when the Russian community got its own church in 1955, there were no pews), and yet, when she came home from it, with tired legs and swollen feet, she had only wonderful things to say about the beauty of the priest's gestures as he swung the incense, about how thoughts were uplifted amid the hymns and the words of the venerable old man.

She was young, she was pretty, she had golden curls that reflected the light at the slightest toss, and she had a determination in her eyes that said that she was happy.

Is it any wonder she created a love so great it could be shared?

During that night when a woman appeared in her husband's soul, she had only a single moment of doubt, and it was in the long silence that followed her question about Jeanne's hat. Hat or no hat, he didn't know what to answer, and she concluded from it, in her impassive quest for happiness, that his flesh had not been affected.

They talked for a long time at the kitchen table. About Jeanne, her speech, the strike, the audience, the story about it that would appear in the *Rouyn-Noranda Press* that my father was to file for the Thursday edition, how to phrase it so that people understood the lumberjacks' cause, how to put into words the brilliance of Jeanne's speech, how everything becomes clear when you hear this woman speak, how Jeanne flushes out the truth, how Jeanne sheds light on our darkest recesses, how Jeanne, how Jeanne, how Jeanne.

The night was long, the hours passed slowly, and when dawn broke, my father had discovered his true feelings. I am in love with this woman, he admitted. My mother didn't falter.

"I know a saint when I see one."

Only once in our theatrical celebrations did we cross the sublimated frontiers of love. Who was playing the paunchy Turnbull-cum-amorous reporter? I believe it was Alexandra, because I have a memory of wild locks of thick black hair escaping from my father's hat just when, having arrived at the head of the bed, she was supposed to collapse as I spoke the final sentence. But Alexandra didn't collapse. She looked at me with a beatific smile and came closer to the bed, and I, driven by what instinct I could not say, leaned toward her because, in spite of the innocence of my five years, I knew we were going to have a kissing scene, the scene we had so hoped for, the kiss that would immortalize Jeanne and our father's love.

But even before we were in position for the kiss (Alexandra and I were in front of one another, our faces practically touching, but we didn't know how to avoid the traffic jam of noses: she tilted right, I tilted right, she tilted left, I tilted left), we heard our mother's soft, cheerful voice say in an almost authoritarian tone, "They didn't kiss."

We quickly moved away from one another, sheepish and a bit ashamed, and our bedroom theatre ended in a great confusion of feelings. One does not kiss a saint.

— Jeanne was not a saint. She was a heroine: a heroine of the Party.

CHAPTER 6

OUR LOVE FOR Jeanne was given to us at birth at the same time as the communist faith and a profound sense of religion. It was a strange concoction that coloured our simplest childhood pleasures with the feeling that life was happening somewhere else.

On that magical night when the angels visited my mother, we became the most spiritually enlightened family on earth.

When I was born ten years later, everything was in place, solidly anchored, and I didn't feel the need to change a thing. I studied the sacred texts with my sisters. We read Marx and Lenin in the literature for the Young Pioneers and the *Clarté*, which our father received at home when it wasn't banned. We read the Old and the New Testaments and handouts our mother brought back from Sunday mass that told of the lives of martyred saints. We read Jeanne's letters, our most treasured moments of reading. And we listened to our father's tales of heroic times.

But our father's heroes weren't always honourable. There were defections, betrayals, and wounds; the passage of time hadn't been easy for the international communist fraternity of our little town.

But we heard about it all, the good and the bad times: the glory days were recounted to us with the same fervour and devotion, no matter whether a comrade fell or the economic climate was hostile. We were spared nothing: nothing was hidden from us. We had intimate knowledge of each of the events of the glory days; we could retell them ourselves in the minutest detail, but we let our father talk, as that was his pleasure and ours. We liked nothing better than gathering around a good communist tale, because we knew that Jeanne would emerge from it, the beautiful and supreme heroine of our hearts.

These moments of family communion normally took place at supper, more precisely over dessert, when we had exhausted the trifling events of the day and someone, most often Alexandra, who couldn't wait any longer for the conversation to turn to weightier matters, asked as if asking about just another thing that had happened that day: "So, Turnbull, did he really read the Riot Act?"

We already knew what happened. We knew the story by heart. Sergeant Turnbull, enemy of the people, had broken up the lumberjack picket line by bringing justice of the peace J. O. Tardif to the scene to read the Riot Act.

The glory days are brimming with moving moments. Aside from the confrontation on the picket line, there were the arrests, the trials, the imprisonments of Jeanne, Donohue, and many others (in total seventy-seven people), and then there was another strike, at the mine this time, the Fros strike, all in less than a year. So there was plenty to choose from.

But the confrontation on the picket line was one of the tastiest morsels of our communist epic. All the snow that fell that day was a godsend, Clara always says, setting a scene of beautiful, white ethereality. The snow was coming down in great sheets that the wind whipped up in gusts and plastered into the faces of our heroes. One hundred and twenty-five men from the forest, sasquatch-like giants, determined not to let anyone pass. They didn't budge when Turnbull arrived with Justice Tardif and a dozen policemen. It was later that things took a turn for the worse.

—Turnbull knew what he was doing bringing the justice of the peace.

He knew, our father explained, that behind their façade of angry giants, there was a long tradition of submission in the hearts of our lumberjacks, and he asked the justice of the peace to read the Riot Act.

The giants were more cowed by the words than they would have been by blows. After the reading of the Riot Act and the sermonizing speech of the justice of the peace, many of them fled into the forest, and those who remained met the police advance without conviction. Not a single shot was fired. Tear gas, which has absolutely no effect in temperatures of minus forty-two degrees, was swept along into the blizzard. The confrontation was fought hand-to-hand and with baton blows.

In less than a half an hour, twelve policemen had quelled a horde of seventy-one enraged men and had lined them up for a long procession to the town hall. Not exactly an image to admire.

"You have to know how to find honour in defeat," Clara said, "hold out hope until victory," and then the heavy boots of the lumberjacks resonated proudly in our ears. It's what we had to retain from the story; it's the lesson our father wanted us to learn. Our heroes, even though they were beaten on the picket line, nonetheless marched the path of glory. They cleared the way so that other workers could take up the fight.

And while glory was taking a long time coming, my sisters and I were waiting for the blizzard to calm, for it to blow itself out and the demurely elegant, very French silhouette of Jeanne to emerge from the white town.

Our father knew how to prolong the pleasure. He knew what we were waiting for, and he gave us a glimpse of everything we loved about Jeanne. First the coat, he would describe the coat. And on that dreamlike white day, Jeanne wore a navy wool coat, a thick, enveloping wool, slightly worn at the elbows, threadbare in spots. The coat hung strait to the knees and was cinched at the waist with a belt in the same wool, knotted once.

"It's the collar that makes the clothes," our mother said.

Since the fragile night when she discovered another woman in her husband's soul, she found out everything about her.

He told her everything, left nothing out, whether or not Jeanne was wearing a hat, whether her skirt was straight or pleated: no detail of Jeanne's appearance was omitted, and if she thought a piece of clothing had been too vaguely described, our mother went straight to the Simpsons-Sears catalogue (women dressed by catalogue in those days), and she would sometimes pick up where my father left off and describe Jeanne's coat collar to us.

"A short-haired fur collar, in deep black beaver or otter, plunging in an elegant crossover."

And so they went, helping one other, down to the fur-lined boots, in the same taupe as the hat, the famous cloche hat that had worried our mother during the night of angels, and yet a hat that was of absolute simplicity. No feathers, no plush fruit on the brim, just a round felt hat, slightly curved on one side, that Jeanne wore to the left in austere coquettishness.

The outfit was not accessorized. Jeanne had no handbag, no satchel of papers, nothing that could hold documents likely to identify her, because it was at the very moment that the blizzard blew out of town leaving it snowy white that she was arrested.

This was the outfit in which our father saw her arrive for her first court appearance, handcuffed and head held high. "Finally," Clara sighed, and we waited for the magical moment when their eyes would meet.

We had not yet come to the long awaited tryst. Jeanne had merely had, in the space of an instant, an intrigued look when a handsome young man — because our father was handsome and distinguished — acknowledged her with a barely perceptible but sustained nod.

She was accused of abetting an unlawful assembly. At issue was her speech. Turnbull quoted long excerpts from it in his testimony, without having taken a single note at the Ukrainian Labour Temple. This always caused a stir in our minds, a mix of perplexity and admiration, because how do you explain a man, caught up in the heat of the action, given so little to abstract thought, who could memorize, intact and complete, words drawn from the purest communist dialectic. "Jeanne's speech touched everyone's heart," one of us finally said. Little girls of the world!

This was not Jeanne's first tangle with the law. She had been arrested four years earlier in Toronto for having led a demonstration in Queen's Park. She was defended by a lawyer from the Canadian Labour Defence League, but that didn't keep her out of jail.

She decided to defend herself this time, to spare the Party the expense, according to Alexandra. It's quite possible. Jeanne was a devoted militant who didn't think of herself; she was probably thinking of Tim Buck and other Communist Party leaders who had been rotting away in the Kingston Penitentiary, and she refused the help that had been unable to save them, the Party greats.

Our mother had a more workaday explanation. She said it was the blizzard that forced our little saint to face adversity alone. The roads were impassable, the train took a day, and none of the flimsy FC-2S that shuttled between Toronto, Rouyn, and Montreal would have risked the storm to drop a lawyer on the ice of Lake Osisko.

Our father didn't search for explanations. He waited until we had finished with our comments to take up the story where a smile had parted her full yet delicate lips to answer the prosecutor's question. She was asked her profession, and Jeanne replied in monotone that she was a teacher. She was asked if her parents lived with her at the address she had given, and she didn't answer. She was a veteran. She knew what you had to give them and what you had to keep for yourself. Communists are constantly before the courts for unlawful assembly, seditious literature, abetting a riot … any pretext will do to lock up a Bolshevik.

In that first court appearance, there was neither a significant exchange of looks nor any other form of a promise. Jeanne left the small courtroom as she had entered: handcuffed but standing tall and proud in spite of the fact that prison awaited her, and our mother didn't raise an eyebrow at the description of the full yet delicate lips.

The Canadian Labour Defence League posted the bond of one thousand dollars, and the Crown stepped up the charges to keep Jeanne in prison, which afforded us a second court appearance and an exchange of looks that, this time, was memorably intense, because my father had found a way to be recognized in the crowd. Jammed between men and women who had come to support our heroine, who was also their heroine — all *foreigners* the *Rouyn-Noranda Press* would write ("Jones edited every one of my stories and reworked them to his liking," he was careful to point out) — he shook his notebook in his outstretched arm, and Jeanne, seeing the young man trying to get her attention, hesitated a moment and then, to our great relief, she recognized him, and the celebrated smile spread, lighting up every muscle of her face, and words could not describe our joy when they acknowledged each other with the same nod of the head.

And this is where our story takes another turn. Enter the Good Samaritan.

Vaara.

He was a titan: he had powerful arms and legs like Hercules. His hands when open were like claws and when closed were like boxing gloves. In spite of his muscle-clad body, he moved like a cat, with a litheness that carried his incredible stature without rippling the air. Slowly, without you noticing, Vaara's lovely great head would look upon you.

— He was a gambler.

My father explained this constant attention to others by Vaara's need to divine their intentions.

— A gambler's mind is always working.

Vaara was indeed a gambler and one of the best. He would win five, six, seven hundred dollars in a single night at poker, and he first appeared in our story with his pockets full of cash.

He was among the throng of *foreigners* who had come to support Jeanne at her second court appearance. He was a Finn and a communist, a diehard, and he became a professional gambler because he was broke after being sacked from the mine for union organizing.

He was among the first to join the struggle. The mine didn't have a gatehouse at that time. People went to show their hands at a logging camp where the manager and the other gentlemen of the mine officiated and slept. When they saw Vaara's two enormous claws open, they immediately assigned him to deep drilling, too pleased with their stroke of luck to notice the newspaper sticking out of his jacket pocket. Although had they done so, they wouldn't have understood anything anyway. It was the *Vapaus*, the official newspaper of the Finnish communist brotherhood in Canada.

Vaara arrived with the great Northern migration, fed by both the revolt that was brewing along the roads and that of his father, who died in the Bolshevik insurrection in Helsinki in 1918, and he carried on his breast a photo of Lenin "like a scapular," our mother would say.

"Lenin is always with us," he would say when we climbed onto his lap and took hold of the shoelace from which the photo hung. Actually, it was my sisters who climbed onto his lap. I wasn't born yet, but I like to share this memory with them. Vaara was a regular visitor to Dallaire Avenue. He came in without knocking, called out hello to whomever was inside, and casually settled in at the table. Clara and

Alexandra would scale the titan's body and search his pockets for the little surprises he brought them.

He was our protector, our adopted uncle, and we adored the moment he first appeared in our story.

Our father hesitated. The two men had fallen out with the years, and he had to go back to who he was at the beginning of their friendship. We knew what that cost him. But when one is a communist, historical truth is sacred. One cannot escape the facts of history laid out in proper perspective, and the historical truth of this friendship that became so bitterly painful was that it was born in the electrically charged courtroom where Jeanne Corbin appeared a second time. So he continued, patient and resigned.

The story was not to our tastes, however; it never was. It was always missing something: it was missing the cap that Vaara kept on his head, while all the other men's heads were bare; it was missing the greetings he extended from one end of the room to the other, the great princely gestures that he offered to one and all; it was missing that movement of the shoulders, a rocking motion that we knew so well and that came from his impatience, a controlled impatience. Vaara was not all muscles and revolt. He knew how to wait, and in this room, there was hope, we who knew the end of the story knew that, and we wanted Vaara's rocking shoulders to be part of the rhythm of the tale. This time, it was Alexandra who asked, "And was Vaara rocking his shoulders?"

Sigh. Exasperation. Silence.

He was accustomed to us interrupting his stories; we did so constantly, but, that, truly, was too much. Too much attention to Vaara annoyed him, and our mother took over, even though she hadn't been in the courtroom, having been too pregnant to put in an appearance, and assured us: "Yes, Vaara rocked his shoulders."

We were reaching Vaara's hour of glory, which our father couldn't stand, and our mother had to tell it in his stead.

The charge had just been read, abetting a riot, and the crowd rose in a clamour of outrage. Jeanne didn't flinch. She had the gentle tranquility of a holy picture. Her iconic smile barely dimmed when the justice of the peace read the charge.

And the shoulder rocking began.

The seriousness of the charge made everyone nervous, except for Vaara, who calms his impatience by rocking his titanic body. He had an ace in his hand, and he was waiting for the right moment to lay down his cards.

— His pockets were stuffed with money.

Vaara had pockets full of money that my father held in contempt with every fibre of his being, and he took out the thick wad like a missal when the justice of the peace read the amount of the bond. Brandishing the wad of bills above his head, his Herculean body cut through the crowd, bills raining down behind him, causing a greater commotion than the announcement of the bond, and he found himself nose-to-nose with the justice of the peace, "the justice perched behind his ambo," our mother said, and we all understood that an ambo is ecclesiastical language for a bench and that Vaara's six feet and then some gave him plenty of height to look deep into the eyes of the judge, while slowly, carefully, maliciously, counting the bills. Two hundred, five hundred, one thousand, two thousand, two thousand five hundred. "Chump change for capitalists," he said, handing over the exact amount.

The best part was that he stayed there and, turning to the crowd, threw a volley of bills along with words that have gone down in history: "A gift from the father of all people." Referring to Stalin, of course.

The crush that followed was just as memorable. People hurled themselves on the manna raining down from above, forgetting the respect due to the courtroom and the men of law, the judge, the prosecutor, and the policemen, all huddled in a ball at the end of the room, appalled, fascinated, and stupefied by this wild outburst of joy celebrating Jeanne's release, the bills landing in cupped hands, the people's victory, the humiliation of men in high places, a brighter future, and the hero of the hour, Vaara, who was looking on, amused.

Amid the cheers, the elbowing, and the joyful hugging and kissing, that sublime moment awaited. We could not forget it in spite of our own joy at the telling of this fleeting, but oh so moving victory of our immigrant friends. Our mother couldn't forget it either as she continued the story, and it was Jeanne who extricated herself from the general merriment to seek out the eyes of the young man, dressed in shabby elegance who so ardently demanded her attention, and, in seeing him, she moved assuredly toward our father, offered her hand, and said in that deep, modulated voice that won the crowds over, "I need to see you."

"Their first tryst," Clara said, and we sighed in unison, because we were all in love with this love, and we knew that finally they would meet in private. Our mother had a very pretty way of consenting to this date.

"God has his moment for the people he chooses."

Dear Mother Courage!

The woman had a flair for happiness. Nothing could tarnish the pleasant succession of days that she wove in our lives. She made joy out of virtually nothing at all: a bird at the window, a prettily decorated cake, or a song on the radio. Every meal was a celebration. No matter what day it was, there was a tablecloth, napkins, and flowers, made from silk stockings, but still very convincing.

Back when Vaara was still welcome at our table, there was also wine and cheese that he brought back from the grocery store owned by the Montemurros, our most illustrious Italians, and an armful of communist literature that he spread out on the tablecloth: books, brochures, scattered leaflets, and what he called his royal flush, the five newspapers published by the Communist Party. Having on hand *The Worker*, *La Vie ouvrière*, *Vapaus*, and that other one with the Ukrainian name that escapes me is one thing, but where on earth did he get his hands on *Der Kampf*? Rouyn Jews were merchants, not communist intellectuals, as far as I know. Be that as it may, the goal of the ethnic literature of the Communist Party was to demonstrate the broad palette of affinities of the great Canadian communist brotherhood.

Vaara had set himself the task of educating our father. The conversations at the table reconstructed the world in the image of a workers' paradise that the Soviet comrades were building in their country, the largest on the planet. Alexandra recalls words that tolled like a bell. Imperialism, capitalism, fascism, Trotskyism. She was at the most six years old at the time, but the galloping weight of those words that did battle at our kitchen table stayed in her head. Marx, Engel, Lenin, Stalin. And sometimes in the midst of the battle, Vaara would shift his bulk toward the little girl sitting sensibly at his side and pick her up as if picking the most beautiful of flowers: "Most Venerable Alexandra," he would say tenderly, almost amorously, and she would find herself nestled in the thick warmth of his arms until late in the evening.

My sister Alexandra was named for Alexandra Kollontai, a Bolshevik, feminist, and libertine in love. Alexandra Kollontai was the People's Commissar in the first Soviet government, but more importantly, in Vaara's heart, she was the person who sustained the Finnish fight for independence. In a way, he knew her personally, because his father, a Finnish revolutionary of pure extraction, had met her many times. "Who knows what happened between them," he liked to hint.

Alexandra Kollontai's love life, magnificently, openly, and consciously free — she wrote at length on the subject — was a great source of pride for Vaara, who himself was an advocate of the unfettered enjoyment of the flesh — and of money, time, and paradise! A new world is on our doorstep, comrade!

It was in the heat of these carryings-on, one evening when they were admiring the world through the lens of the revolutionary theories of Alexandra Kollontai, that Vaara, pointing to our mother's round belly, uttered the words that would destine my sister to carry the name of that venerable woman: "It will be a girl, and she will be a great communist and a great lover."

This was at the start of their friendship, and our father didn't think twice about taking my sister to the baptismal font with a name that proudly proclaimed his new convictions.

When another child was announced a few months later, the two men talked for long evenings, searching for the one who could preside over its destiny. So when the child turned out to be a girl, the name of another great feminist revolutionary awaited her: Clara, for Clara Zetkin, militant communist emeritus, journalist, orator, and also a great lover. She too was loved by a man much her junior, although she was a woman of austere appearance, whereas Alexandra Kollontai loved jewellery, furs, and stylish clothes.

"Most Venerable Alexandra" and "Illustrious Little Clara." They formed a pair in Vaara's arms and in life. They were inseparable, even after a fight, even at school (they were in the same class, Alexandra having repeated grade four), even through the dating years. They both married Ukrainian men from our neighbourhood, Dan and Panko, who took them to St. Catharines in Southern Ontario, where they squandered their ideological heritage in department stores. I was the only one left. And my father took me with him on the road.

CHAPTER 7

— A TURNCOAT.

I don't know how Vaara slipped into the conversation, but he wouldn't be allowed to stay there long. His name doesn't appear anywhere in my notebooks, not even when the stories are about him, like this time, explicitly and accidentally. I could have written it down — no one was looking over my shoulder — but I stuck to my role: I stayed with my father's thoughts, and in the unrelenting passage of time, the grudge had not waned, and Vaara's name had to be obliterated.

— A turncoat, a hedonist, and a rebel.

THE EPITHETS STREAMED forth, always the same ones. One, two, three. Turncoat, hedonist, rebel. Once I heard the first, I knew that I would hear the second and the third. A bitter threesome in tribute to a lost friendship.

I knew too that he wanted me to understand.

He had worked his way up to a pinnacle of thought from which you can see all of humanity and its history, and from that vantage point he had started to hope for a glorious march, an irrepressible, unremitting advance, with all of humanity in the grips of a single movement, history marching toward the appearance of a New Man. You don't just abandon a doctrine that offers so much hope. Vaara the turncoat had turned his back on it when the Soviets invaded Finland in 1939.

My father's rancour was all the more bitter because it was Vaara, the gambler and turncoat, who had initiated him to communism, in those endless conversations that started at our kitchen table and continued late into the night in the basement of the Hôtel Radio, where my father had his office and Vaara his gambling house. They were adjacent, and although one was completely respectable and the other entirely illicit, they were similarly dark and smoky, and could easily be confused so scarce was the air and so thick was the silence among the men holed up in them. The movement of cards on the table and the hammers of the Remington on the blank page: it was the same enchantment, the same reverence. The policemen who came to raid the gambling house sometimes got the wrong place in the dark and burst in to the offices of the *Rouyn-Noranda Press*, giving those on the other side of the wall plenty of time to run. The town really was a bit of a joke.

Was Vaara more of a rebel than a communist? That's what my father claimed, he who, all of his life, had respect only for professional revolutionaries. In the 1970s, when new ideas turned the town on its head once again, I had a great deal of empathy for the young people who dragged their long-haired views through the bars. I was looking for love and consuming passion, and I followed the boys until my father's voice became too insistent.

— They're Vaaras. They're all Vaaras.

Those boys drew me like honey. I loved their long languid strides, their legs stretching and retracting endlessly on the concrete sidewalk. I loved how they tossed back their hair. I loved the scent they trailed behind them. I liked to follow them wherever they went and listen to them expound. They were in love with freedom and justice, they were ready for a fight, they were going to change the world, and I loved their arms, their legs, their hands, their mouths, their scent, and their beds, until I could no longer hear my father, who was already gone, but who had never stopped whispering in my head.

— All Vaaras, incapable of a real commitment, only interested in their own pleasure, false stars who are fleeting and flimsy.

Vaara was nothing more than a hedonist in my father's eyes.

— A hedonist and a gambler.

His rancour made him forget that the money so easily won in the town's gambling houses — because there were many and Vaara went from house to house so as not to try the patience of the gamblers with his uncanny talent — would find its way to our table. Vaara won a fortune, but he settled for a rundown room at the Nickel Range Hotel and a jacket he wore until the leather stuck to his skin; in short, the same life he led as a miner, except for the ladies of the night, whom he rewarded handsomely, and the rounds of drinks that won him a gang of rowdy friends. The rest went to the Canadian Labour Defence League, the Finn Hall, the Ukrainian Labour Temple, anyone in town who was a communist, poor, helpless, and outraged, and we received our share. The money arrived, regularly and discreetly, in an envelope that Vaara slid under his napkin, and it paid the electricity bills, the rent, our tab at the grocery store, almost everything needed to keep a family, because D.A. Jones didn't tolerate a communist journalist in his inner circle for very long, and my father found himself available for a life of battle for the liberation of the people.

But he would never call himself a professional revolutionary.

— A true revolutionary has no other life but the Party.

And we would come back to Jeanne Corbin, obviously, our Jeanne who was the winsome inspiration for this way of thinking.

— Jeanne wasn't looking for honours or simple pleasures. She wanted only the depth of feeling of a life well lived.

We were driving alongside a river that had been calm and gentle for miles and that was now swollen and turbulent. I watched it rise along the road, and I said to myself that life is like that, sometimes gentle and serene, sometimes stormy, with a current you have to follow. My father never had those sorts of thoughts.

We had done two villages up to that point. Two sleepy villages brought out of their torpor by our arrival, just long enough to be astonished by us, me, the young girl with the unrelenting smile, and my father, master of word and gesture. First, he went into a store, a garage, or a post office — who can say, it's all a blur, the people, the things, the dust, the shadow, and the light — and I was behind him, a pile of newspapers in my arms, waiting for the first greetings to be exchanged. From the tone of the rumblings that greeted us, I could guess whether there would be caustic, mocking, or hostile words, whether my father would parry the attacks, deflect the jokes, move minds to new horizons, whether we would manage to leave our newspapers behind on consignment or whether we would have to make a run for it.

I don't really have any bad memories of our travels. On the contrary, I feel like a privileged witness to the passing of a comet. The people in those villages had so little opportunity to be amazed.

After the two villages, we ate a hearty meal on the side of the road. We stayed in the car, because it was spring and was damp everywhere, and there was nowhere to spread our tablecloth.

Sometimes during our short stops, he would let himself be transported by thoughts that had nothing to do with anything, long ramblings that came and went in waves and that I captured as best I could in my notebooks. This tumultuous material perplexes me. I don't know what to make of it.

Love was what swept everything along, the groundswell of these long soliloquies that punctuated our travels with a touch of surrealism, because love is adoration, sublimation, and the sacred road to a reality where the essence of life itself is found. That other kind of love, the love that embraces you, coddles you, makes you go zip-a-dee-doo-dah and how-sweet-it-is-being-loved, can make you happy only if you have access to the sacred way. Dear Mother Courage kept both forms of love alive to preserve her own!

After the picnic in the car, we travelled east, toward the sawmills and the men in the forest, the lumberjacks who were so dear to my father's heart. The great days of communism were long past; the lumberjacks of the 1960s weren't the same as those of the glory days, but hope stays the course, nostalgia holds the road.

—They'll listen, you'll see. They're going to hear what I have to say, and you'll see the fire in their eyes. You'll see the resistance rise up. They won't accept exploitation and humiliation any longer.

So many times I had seen him booed by crowds of men who could have beaten him to a pulp but who settled for merely laughing, applauding at the wrong time, making fun, hissing, being coarse and mocking. Big tall men, at home in their fortress of muscles. They could have crushed my father's head under their thumbs, but they did nothing. It was their form of civility, I suppose, in exchange for which they could scoff all they wanted.

All my father needed in order to believe that this sideshow was worthwhile was for the eyes of one of the lot to light up. If one person for the tiniest moment had the slightest show of intelligence, a spark in his eye, my father felt that he had saved the world from wilful ignorance.

These were the moments of inspiration that kept us on the road. We went from village to village, arms filled with newspapers, that were accepted or declined, and if by chance we arrived as mass let out or during a fair, auction, or any sort of event, we would pull out a rough wooden box from the trunk of the car, an old vegetable crate that served as his pulpit, and after a brief study of the site, he would set up in the middle of the throng, standing on his box, and address the crowd, managing to gain their attention after a few false starts.

It pained me to see him exposed to ridicule that way. But I know it made him happy, yes, happy to have his shot at stirring up hope for a new day like the great orators of the glory days, and the crowd's merriment changed nothing. I would be by his side with my pile of newspapers, and I would watch him be swept away, go red in the face and soar beyond time, and I knew for certain, both thrilled and alarmed, that after a certain passage I would hear *The laws are just papier mâché created by a bourgeoisie that doesn't know what it is to work with sweat on their brow*, and then *Gone are the times when workers must bleed themselves dry to put food on the tables of the rich*, words taken from the famous speech at the Ukrainian Labour Temple, and the illusion would be complete. He would see himself surrounded by ardent militants, a motley crowd, with colourful headscarves, embroidered shirts, and thick felt berets, rather than this uniformly indolent and insolent crowd in a square in front of a country church.

I heard him say at the end of a gloomy afternoon when cattle farmers were gathered in a sun-scorched field (a baseball tournament or a picnic, I don't remember which), *If there are not enough men on the picket lines, the women will join them.*

He had never left the room where he was given those words.

We drove further east still, northeast in fact, where the great mythical forest lay. We had never been, but I knew that the illusion would be perfect. Hundreds of men in the woods gathered around him, their smell of sap intermingled with rivers of sweat, their attentive, muscular presence ... he would definitely be transported back to that room where he was born again when he was a young journalist. He wanted to bring the moment when everything was given to him back to life.

He never moved on from that time, that town, the person he was. He believed that everything was a matter of will, that with time and militant patience, he would once again find his cherished Ukrainian Labour Temple somewhere along the road, and if the crowds of poor people we met were lacking in hope, we had to go farther, to where the heirs to the glory days would be found, where there was no shortage of courage and heroism, among the lumberjacks in the northern forest. He was on his way to meet a great moment in his life.

And then the car broke down.

My father was completely hopeless with this sort of thing, and when the car suddenly declared it could go no farther, I told myself I would have to play it smart, because it was going to take money to fix it.

Luckily, we weren't far from a town, and we could see a first row of roofs below a wooded area into which the river wound.

— It's the carburetor.

He would say whatever came into his head.

— The valve is blocked and the carburetor's choked. Yes, that's it, it's the carburetor. It's not getting air and it choked.

He was under the hood, pretending to know his way around the hunks of metal. He tapped on the engine, stretched a belt, unscrewed the gas cap, his hands moving here and there, incompetent, clumsy, ignorant, completely useless: they didn't understand a thing they were touching.

— It could be the transmission belt, but it's not old. Unless it's the cylinder block. It looks clogged to me.

It was time for me to deliver him from this humiliating dance of hesitation.

— I'm going to go get a tow truck.

— Yes, I think that's the only thing for it.

— I'll go call.

We both knew that we didn't have the money for a tow truck or a mechanic.

— Tell him that I've tried everything and that there's nothing we can do. This clunker just won't start.

I would call Vaara. I would explain. I would ask him to talk to the mechanic, and he would take care of everything. Vaara was rich by this point; he had hotels all over the place. His name was enough to get any of his friends out of a jam, and we were still friends, in spite of what my father may have thought.

—Tell him that I'll pay him back as soon as I can.

I was already halfway down the road. His voice reached me intermittently. I could hear him ranting and raving, but I couldn't make out his words. He was throwing all of his bitterness toward his lost friend into the wind.

CHAPTER 8

THE GLORY DAYS lasted only one year. From December 9, 1933, when Jeanne made her speech at the Ukrainian Labour Temple, until her imprisonment at Ville Marie, only a year had passed. Twelve months during which the town held its breath as the events rushed by until there was nothing left of them, absolutely nothing: Rouyn has no memory of a time when it was red.

Sometimes I feel like I was born somewhere else.

Nothing remains of the Finn Hall or the Ukrainian Labour Temple. The places that fed my childhood with incredible stories no longer exist. The two men who had crossed their wrists in blood and lifted them high to salute "The Internationale." The woman who unbuttoned her blouse crying "Long live the revolution." The other woman who brought her husband's arm, torn off in a rockslide at the mine, and who stood on the podium calling for vengeance. The short man, hairy as an ape, ugly as sin, and almost voiceless, who held the audience spellbound until the wee hours with the wonders he had seen in the USSR. The unbearable deafening clamour, the roar of thunder that greeted the miners' strike vote. The long vigils during the strike and the daring plans to escape Turnbull and his minions. And Jeanne, getting lighter and lighter in her dress, paler and paler, who came to support them, leaving again for another cause to defend, in Timmins, in Hearst, in Thunder Bay, and coming back with reinforcements, a Party dignitary, a lumberjack who had seen the strike in Spruce Falls, always on the go, a whirlwind getting paler, frailer, more heart-rending, and our father who waited for her return.

That heroic year was the year of the lumberjacks' strike; the miners' strike; confrontations in the street; D.A. Jones's vitriolic editorials and humiliation; strikes brutally, ignominiously, and savagely broken; and our father driven out of the *Rouyn-Noranda Press*.

My sisters and I followed the accounts of "the year of great hope," as our father called it, waiting for each of Jeanne's appearances, wondering which would end in a tryst, which would finally consecrate the love that we so devotedly kept alive.

The year of the tryst, that's what we called it.

No matter what incident was recounted to us, we waited for the moment when he would sidle up to her and arrange a meeting. It would be a moment of such beautiful intensity. He would be shy, terror-stricken by what he was about to ask, and he would slip into the crowd, because she was always surrounded by supporters and militants (lovers? he would wonder). The panic would peak when, drawing near her, he would pull out his notepad and pencil and ask her his first questions, but there would come a moment when there was no more point in clinging to his role as a reporter. He would run out of questions, his voice would crack, he would feel everything slipping away from him, and in a state of panic, he would ask her.

Trysts normally took place at the Imperial Café, a restaurant on Noranda Street run by a Chinese man. He described the setting every time (a row of booths along each wall, a counter at the back, bare, greying planks everywhere, the floorboards barely planed), which wasn't all that important, because it was the dress we were waiting for. Jeanne arrived at the appointed time, removed the familiar coat to reveal the day's outfit, which was not a dress in fact, but an ensemble, a blouse and a skirt in matching colours, always in tones of navy and charcoal grey, brightened up once in a while with a detail that he would describe to us precisely. A row of tiny glass buttons on the blouse, a belt with a big buckle, a lace-trimmed collar: these were what held our attention. Oh, the collars! Tailored collars! Draped collars! Bow collars! Petal collars! Ruched collars. Collars were the jewels of Jeanne's wardrobe.

— She was not an uptown piece of fluff, he never failed to point out, but a militant, a heroine of the Party.

The day's fashions offered women of modest means a range of detachable collars that allowed them to change their outfit without really changing it. This was why Jeanne, a modest militant but a woman nonetheless, almost always appeared to us in the same blouse, but made the effort to adorn it with a collar that we welcomed each time with the same rapturous comments. We knew them all. The rayon taffeta collar with a ruched bow, the rough crepe collar trimmed with lace, the tailored collar lined with a v-neck frill. The year of great hope was teeming with events: there were communist assemblies every other week at the labour temples, and most of the time Jeanne was the guest speaker, so we got to know all of the detachable collars in her wardrobe.

We each had our favourite. Mine was the collar from the first meeting. Lying closer to the neck than a Peter Pan collar, it still had a childlike roundness, and it had just the right amount of lace trim. We knew it well, because that first tryst was disappointing and, rather than weighing ourselves down in the details of the story that would disappoint us even more, we asked our father to tell us more about what Jeanne was wearing when she arrived at the *Rouyn-Noranda Press*, because that was where the first meeting took place. She was accompanied by the small man with the unflappable smile, Joseph Ellinuk, local secretary of the Workers' International Relief. The infamous Jones was also there. There was nothing romantic about it: the sole purpose of the meeting was the events taking place. Jeanne had come to make a statement. We concentrated on the collar that was milky white against the charcoal grey of the blouse.

Jeanne was accompanied by the little man to refute, figures in hand, the dreadful things that D.A. Jones was saying in his editorials. He had written that the lumberjacks' strike was stirred up by foreign agitators on Moscow's payroll, and that these henchmen of international communism couldn't care less about the lumberjacks and were only after the fall of the capitalist democracy that had so generously welcomed them, them and their ilk. The most despicable lie concerned the strike fund. Jeanne had come to show that, contrary to Jones's accusations, the money came from donations and was used strictly to feed and house the strikers.

Jeanne was dazzling. We listened to our father's tale and again admired her incredible energy. The strike was a total failure. The lumberjacks went back to the forest; seventy-seven of them were in prison. Jeanne herself was facing a charge of abetting a riot and there she was, arguing, waving papers and numbers about to convince the loathsome Jones that the strike had not been financed by the Comintern.

But we were disappointed. That first tryst should have been pure romance, and yet we were still deep in the territory of ideological war.

We concentrated on the full yet delicate lips, the intermittent smile, the collar with its milky whiteness, and the fact that Jones would fall under her spell. That's what our mother said at the end of the story. Jones fell under her spell. She backed up our father throughout the tale, and when he had to end it, she was the one who came to his rescue, putting a comforting hand on his arm and saying, as if the words had been dictated to her from beyond: "And Jones fell under her spell." And that made everything all right. We had returned to Jeanne as a private person, to that subtle power she had of drawing people in: we had returned to the territory of seduction.

"Jones fell under her spell, and from that moment on, he could hardly write Jeanne's name without adding an adjective that praised her for her courage, her gentleness, or her beauty."

Jones became part of the magic circle of Jeanne's admirers. "Nobody could resist Jeanne's charm," our mother repeated. So there we were, united with Jones(!) in our adoration of the halo of pure beauty that encircled our saint's forehead. Dear Mother Courage!

It's true that after that meeting, the *Rouyn-Noranda Press* was much more conciliatory toward Jeanne, even though it continued to launch blistering attacks on communism, foreigners, the labour temples, and their supporters. I have read every issue of the *Rouyn-Noranda Press* from the glory days, and there is a clear difference between the violent and vituperative Jeanne of the earlier issues and the young woman of delicate, demure appearance that followed. The petite French woman, you can read between the lines, touches the heart, even though she is defending, *valiantly*, he wrote, indefensible positions. As the events unfolded, the newspaper worried about a cough that prevented her from continuing her speech, and then it was the young woman's thinness that became cause for concern, her increasing pallor, with disease lurking in the subtext and endearing her even more.

I read all of these stories on microfilm. We are fortunate enough to have a national archives office in our little city, a pleasant place where I followed the strange duel that united Jones and my father.

The archives office is located where the Montemurro grocery store used to be. I like to think that the newspapers of those epic days are preserved at the very place where Vaara went to get the cheese and sausage for our table. I was familiar with Vaara's sausages only through the stories I was told, and yet I can imagine the smell of them amid the archive shelves. A strong garlicky smell, "a communist smell," our mother would say, for she believed that anyone who wore a red armband and a scapular of Lenin, anyone who knew that hands that toil are hands that hope, would be an ardent eater of garlic sausage.

So surrounded by wafts of garlic, I looked for the kindly adjectives among the articles for four hands that D.A. Jones and my father wrote. Because that was how it worked. My father went to the event, took notes, wrote a first draft and Jones took everything, the notes and the draft, and concocted an article of his own devising.

The first kind words for Jeanne appeared in the January 4, 1934 issue, one week after the meeting at the *Rouyn-Noranda Press*. She was described as a *frail* young woman. One senses all of the writer's attention when she spoke at the Finn Hall, which was filled to the rafters. *Two-hundred and fifty people raised the roof with their applause*, he wrote.

— Jones was in the room.

Yes, Jones was in the room! That's how incredible Jeanne's power was. After the meeting at the *Rouyn-Noranda Press*, D.A. Jones could stay away no longer, and he would find himself in the labour temples any time Jeanne was to make an appearance.

Thus began the strange duel. Jones, the highly detestable and much detested, sat on a straight-backed chair surrounded by comrades, and my father roamed the crowd, notebook in hand. Jones watched, listened, soaked up the ambiance, but didn't take notes. My father handled that. He transcribed the slogans on the blackboard, transcribed the chorals young girls sang during the entertainment portion of the evening, transcribed speeches verbatim, except for Jeanne's, which went directly to his soul. When she made her way to the podium, the two men glanced sidelong at each other, and then, nothing more: they forgot one another. Jeanne's voice had swelled in the room. The next day, when they compared notes on the evening for the article to appear in the paper, my father would be astonished to learn that not a single word of Jeanne's speech had escaped his boss, that he could even pinpoint when her voice had derailed and when the dry, hoarse cough, which came two sentences later, had begun.

Jeanne's speech had touched D.A. Jones in the same impenetrable places as it had my father.

We tried to transpose this strange relationship that united the two men to our bedroom theatre. Me, standing on the bed, Clara in our father's old overcoat, and Alexandra seated on the straight-backed chair. But there was no point, we couldn't manage it. Too many things escaped us.

We played the scene only once, but it is burned in my mind. The image of Alexandra/Jones is particularly unforgettable. My sister didn't know whether she should move or stay glued to her chair, whether she should look enraptured, admiring, or coldly contemplative, whether she should hint at being in love, whether there should be pain in the emotion or bliss, whether this was a tortured or a happy man. It was a gripping, kaleidoscopic haze. We never knew whether Jones was truly in love with Jeanne.

"The Lord works in mysterious ways."

Our mother placed her trust in God and followed our father's loves as if they were her own.

The second tryst took place at the Imperial Café, alone in the private booth in the back, a steaming coffee in their hands, and the notebook lying inert at the centre of the table. Once again, my father would forget to take notes.

The trysts at the Imperial Café went pretty much the same way. Jeanne would arrive at the appointed time; my father would have been waiting for a half an hour. She would take off her coat or her cardigan or nothing at all (the meetings took place in all seasons). My father would mentally record the details of her outfit, and then one or the other of them would let out a laugh, a nervous one if it were my father, and a light, tinkling one if it were Jeanne (she was laughing and cheerful in private), and the conversation would begin, a bit awkwardly at first, but they would soon come to what my father and the rest of us had been waiting for: the story of her life.

I don't know how he managed to draw so many confidences from a woman so little given to introspection.

"She was moved by your father's great mind."

My mother believed that the best of people is found in the upper reaches of the mind and that this was where the meetings took place.

When he returned from the Imperial Café, it was the more worldly aspects off the meeting that interested her, however. Did Jeanne have the flu? Was she wearing the flattering crepe collar? Was she wearing glasses? At what point did she take them off? As for Jones, he tracked the communist germ that had infected Jeanne's life. After my mother's questions came Jones's, because my father would then go to the newspaper office, and, under the pretext of the article they were writing together, Jones wanted to know everything. Whether there were Bolsheviks among the farmers of Cellettes or a communist lover somewhere in her Albertan youth. How did one become a Marxist when one was so young, beautiful, intelligent, and destined for a contented life in a country that had so much to offer? But he also asked after Jeanne's health. Did she get weak or have a coughing fit during the interview?

What interested my sisters and I was young Jeanne, the five-year-old who crossed the Atlantic on a ship a hundred times the size of a house.

I sometimes think that in telling the story so often, my father was robbed of his moments of intimacy with Jeanne.

The trysts at the Imperial Café were followed with a passion, devotion, and meticulousness that never flagged when a detail of the story resisted. My valiant mother never gave up inquiring when presented with a vague account. She would go to the Simpsons-Sears catalogue and find the detachable collar that she had been unable to identify in our father's report.

During the year of great hopes, my mother was perpetually pregnant with my sisters, a condition that forced women of the era into almost total reclusion, so she could only acquaint herself with the detachable collars through my father's descriptions and what she could glean from the catalogue.

But there was one episode during the glory days that, while it could be hardly be called a meeting, had afforded my mother a glimpse of Jeanne, from afar and without her knowing, it's true, and one that remained hazy in all the accounts I managed to squeeze out of her. For a long time I was reluctant to believe it.

I only discovered the existence of the episode through one of my father's reflections. We were on the road, and we had picnicked in the car again, on account of a mid-July hail storm. As it sometimes happened, when we were confined for a long time to the stillness of the road, he was soliloquizing to his heart's content, paying no attention to me, and amid the muddle of ideas that came out of him, there was this sentence.

— It wasn't the dress of a woman in love.

I know how to recognize Jeanne's presence when she passes. For my father, she manifested herself through a dilation of the pupils that gave him a dazed look. It would generally last just a few seconds, but it was long enough to tell me that Jeanne would emerge from it. This time, his pupils had dilated to an astonishing level, and I got scared. I asked him if he felt all right, if he needed air, if I should get him some water. He shook his head.

— Don't worry. She wasn't in love with Jones.

What he said to me then did nothing to reassure me, because he was lost in a stream of words from which I couldn't pry free the least bit of reason. It was about the imminent release of Tim Buck, about a big gathering that was to take place, about Jones having tricked him, about Jeanne, whom he hadn't seen. Yes, finally, he saw her, but it was impossible, and that dress she was wearing — how could she? I didn't know which end of this gibberish to grab, to tease out if only a thin thread of an explanation, so I clung to the dress. What colour was it?

— Red, blood-red, revolution-red, not love-red, he answered in a single breath. She was not in love with Jones.

And then he dove back into the stormy sea. The thoughts that rattled him were increasingly insistent, increasingly confused, but somewhere in the storm, I understood that Jeanne had had a private meeting with Jones.

A private meeting, at the Imperial Café, in a fiery red dress, without my father knowing, Jones having sent him on a wild goose chase. That's what I managed to extract from everything he didn't want to tell me on the subject.

The hail stopped, the storm calmed, we got back on the road, and the conversation meandered here and there. The ghostly meeting came back to haunt our travels only on rare occasions.

I understand that the meeting couldn't be told as part of a logical story. I'm only a witness from afar myself; I've managed to grasp only the flimsiest of fragments.

On his way back from his goose chase, my father passed in front of the Imperial Café (the restaurant looked onto Noranda Street through a window caked with dirt but transparent nonetheless) and saw Jeanne deep in conversation with a man in the back booth, at the very spot where they had had their own meeting. He looked closer. She was wearing a magnificent red dress, a fluttering blaze of fabric that opened into a corolla at the base of the neck, a dress that he had never seen before. As he looked closer, he realized that the man in front of her was none other than Jones. My father didn't understand. What was she doing there, at the Imperial Café? There was nothing going on that could explain her being in Rouyn, even less so with Jones, who was not a habitué of the café, of meetings with women or of intimate conversations with Jeanne, and she was not in the habit of wearing flamboyant clothes. And then came the most incredible part.

"He asked me, begged me, to go see."

Had my mother not told me it was true, I would never have believed it, so hard was it to imagine the shut-in dashing out of the house, her pregnancy weighing in her step as she walked along Noranda Street, and then peering through the window. "Jeanne was definitely there with Jones, but I couldn't see the dress properly because the Chinese man had brought coffee, and he was in the way." She went down as far as Avenue du Lac and backtracked as if she had forgotten something, getting in another glance in passing. "She was much prettier than I had imagined, the face of a Madonna. There was a self-awareness in her that stirred me deep inside, and the dress was truly magnificent." She went home with an increasingly pregnant step (Clara was born three months later) to bring the good news to my father who was waiting at the apartment.

"That wasn't the dress of a woman in love."

The words had the desired effect, I suppose, and reassured my father, because they resurfaced often during the long sermons on the road, like a balm to unruly thoughts.

For a long time I didn't know what to make of the strange jumble of feelings that must have sustained them, my father asking my mother to check whether the woman who had bewitched him was in fact under the spell of another man, and my mother, completely devoted to love, both hers and the love that her husband kept alive for another woman, heading out on a quest he had set for her and finding that dress to offer him, a red dress, which was clearly not a colour Jeanne was in the habit of wearing, but that would reassure them forever more, because it was with the same relief that they repeated to one another, each time I tried to come back to the story, that it was not the dress of a woman in love.

I asked Vaara about it. The Soviets had not yet invaded Finland, and he was still a close friend of our father's and a frequent guest at our table around the time of the scarlet dress.

He made the same gesture he always did when I asked him to untangle the threads of the story. He lifted his powerful shoulders, formed from the thick play of muscles at the nape, and let them fall while opening his arms. A gesture of grief or resignation, I'm not sure which, followed by a worn-out sigh, "Little One, let it be." He still called me "Little One" at the ages of thirty, forty, and fifty, as if I were still the person he had stuffed with sweets when I went to see him behind my father's back at the hotel on Avenue Principale or the one on Gamble Street, because he owned several.

"Little One …," and he would go to great lengths to explain the backdrop to the story. He has character and breath to spare, our Vaara, and he likes to let the full length of a story unfold before making his point.

The great hopes had died, the miners' strike was broken, even more savagely than the lumberjack strike, with arrests, prison, and deportations. The labour temples would soon be the stuff of folklore, and only by looking far off into the distance could a communist soul still have hope. The Canadian authorities had in fact just announced the impending release of comrades from the Kingston Penitentiary, and Jeanne was celebrating in that little red dress. She had arrived from Timmins, where they had had a party for a comrade who had just been released, and she wanted to convince Jones to write an article about it. And the dress? The dress that opened so magnificently into a corolla? "She probably bought it for the comrade's party in Timmins, and she was wearing it just like she would any other. She was not the sort of woman who would wear a dress only once."

Vaara tends to throw a harsh light onto reality, while I look for the glow of the depths. What was the point of equilibrium between the fragile threesome? My mother, with a love so great that she would put up with my father's love for another woman? My father, transported by a feeling so strong that it had to be shared? Did Jeanne ever know the commotion caused by her presence at the Imperial Café? "Little

One, leave well enough alone," and his shoulders would sag. This wasn't a story he took pleasure in.

I believe that my parents were both refined in their thinking in a way that precluded the idea of rivalry. Neither of them would have allowed themselves to descend into the arena of love and fight with a feeling as vile as jealousy. I inherited this tendency to believe that I'm above my own feelings, and I have chalked up my fair share of loves that couldn't be.

But the question of Jones still remained. The man had a particular place on the list of people we abhorred; because while he was an enemy of the people, and not a minor one at that, he had been touched by Jeanne's grace, and that fact alone made him someone who deserved special treatment. This was not the case, for example, for Turnbull, who was the incarnation of absolute evil, a man who was held in contempt, reviled, and thoroughly ridiculed in our bedroom theatre.

Jones was a man of great intellectual vigour. I read all the writings from those glory days. He could address any topic with equal competence in his page-four editorial: the rise of Nazism in Germany or the relocation of the farmer's market on Gamble Street. He had a documented opinion for everything and an incredible instinct for dealing with events that threatened free enterprise, the social order, and Christian values. D.A. Jones was, however, a xenophobe of the worst kind, vitriolic without burdening himself with intellectual effort as soon as an immigrant appeared in one of his articles.

How could such a man sit for hours in the middle of a crowd that was hostile to him? Sometimes our friends at the labour temples would boo and even shove him. I read about it in the March 22, 1934 issue.

Was Jones in love with Jeanne? The question never came up as bluntly as that and was never satisfactorily answered in any of the stories from the glory days, even the last one, as laden in meaning as the story of the scarlet dress was, and as murky, because we never knew whether Jones let our father go in a fit of lover's pique or an attack of ideological rage.

It happened in December 1934. Jeanne's trial was just over, and she was en route for the Ville Marie Jail and, in the police car that stopped at the gas station on Larivière Avenue, there were two men with her in the backseat. Jerry Donohue and Ludovic Sopsic. Donohue had been sentenced to six months in prison, Sopsic to eighteen months and Jeanne got off with three months. The charge of abetting a riot had been reduced to participating in an unlawful assembly, but it was her presence, the softness and the sadness of her voice, that had earned her the judge's compassion.

I read the report of the trial in the *Gazette du Nord*, a newspaper from Amos, because that was where it took place, and I wasn't surprised that they fell in love with Jeanne the moment they saw her. The journalist who covered the trial (the article had no byline, so I don't know who he was) was also touched by Jeanne's grace. The report was enough to make you cry. It was an impressionist piece in which the anonymous journalist was touched, felt compassion, but never raised a single fact or a single argument presented by any party. He was interested only in Jeanne. *She made her arguments at the end of a very grey day. Her face, her voice, and her arguments were grey. There was a feeling of great sadness about the scene.*

Jeanne must have truly been in a sorry state. *She looked ominously tubercular*, the grief-stricken reporter wrote, and it makes me want to weep with him.

He fell under her spell, my mother would have said had she read it, and the grief-stricken reporter would have joined the magic circle where she gathered all those who shared the same love for Jeanne. I think this is how to understand her determination to preserve her happiness in a sweeping ecumenical love.

I am coming to the final tableau of the glory days, the scene at the gas station, because Jones, in his article about the event, was also alarmed by Jeanne's state of health.

She was thin, very thin, emaciated in fact, obviously suffering from a bad flu, and she was surprised, and smiled wanly, when Jones inquired about her health. She was in the backseat beside the door, and they talked quietly. She said that she didn't understand what she had been accused of, that she had done nothing wrong, but that she would continue her work in prison, and the story ended when she asked him for a hot coffee for the road. It would be the last time she would appear in the *Rouyn-Noranda Press*.

What interests me is what Jones didn't write. There are a number of things that need clarifying; for example, how Jones ended up there at the very moment the police car stopped, and, even more intriguing, how my father had slipped into the front seat between the two policemen. Maybe he was already there and Jones only noticed it when he came back with Jeanne's coffee. And even more troubling than these details is that it was after the scene in the car that my father first disappeared.

So Jones came back with a coffee for Jeanne and discovered my father between the two policemen.

What happened next has fallen into the great nebula of my father's disappearances. When he came back ten days later, thinner, haggard, and with a steady determination in his eyes, he simply told our mother that he had been fired and that a new life was beginning.

"And happiness was returned to me."

CHAPTER 9

I LOOKED THROUGH many photos at the archives office. The men, when they weren't posing, all look like laid-back cowboys; when they were, they stared down the camera with an incredible intensity. The long-haired boys that I later followed through the same streets also had that way of trailing something indefinably proud and nonchalant behind them.

In one photo, I saw two men walking quietly down the middle of a road, their steps weighed down by large boots laced up to the knees, one smoking a cigarette and the other with one hand in his pants pocket, tracing a large movement with the other, elegant gestures in spite of the weight of their clothing, the mud on the road, the wooden sidewalks on piles, and the colourlessness of the buildings that frame the photo. The two men are not identified. They could be prospectors, Byelorussians talking about their country, or hobos just off the train. They have the effortlessness of freedom that this town offers.

There are very few women in the photos for the simple reason that there were very few women in Rouyn. I tried to find Jeanne, without much hope I must say, but had she appeared in the photos, I would have recognized her without ever having seen her. She was nowhere to be found among the women smiling at the photographer. No sign of the velvety eyes or the full yet delicate lips.

I spotted Turnbull, a strapping man posing with other policemen in the middle of Eighth Street during the miners' strike. Behind them are the smokestacks of the mine against a chalky sky and, gathered on either side of the street, the miners and their families, who you can tell are watchful, worried, anxious. Turnbull, on the other hand, gives off an air of calm assurance. He's in control of the situation. You can feel it; you can see it in how he stands, legs slightly apart, hands clasped, and that look that will not back down.

He left town a few years later to become a purchasing manager or some such thing for a mine in Ontario. It was Marthe, the archivist at the office of archives, who told me. There was no trace of him after that. He killed himself, according to Marthe. I hardly know what to think: this man we took so much pleasure in hating may have been tormented, slowly consumed by a monster within, maybe even while the events that gave us reason to hate him were taking place.

Things are not as simple when it comes to Jones, who I also looked for amid the archive photos, not knowing whether he was bald, moustachioed, moon-faced, bespectacled or not. These details were overlooked in the tales of the glory days.

We thought of nothing but love at the time, True Love, the kind that hovered over Jeanne, and we never thought to ask whether Jones was young or old, handsome or ugly.

Jones plagued the pages of the *Rouyn-Noranda Press* long after those days. After the miners' strike, he was able to pour out his vitriol at his leisure. The strike agitators were immigrant workers, the *foreigners* he so loathed in his heart. They had been fired or deported, and those who remained no longer walked as freely in the streets. Jones's hateful propaganda had the desired effect. The town changed course. Gone was the beautiful and languorous Slav nonchalance, making way for a parking lot, as the singer says. The town forgot that it had ever been red.

I looked through the photos in the archives for a place on Larivière Street that could have been where the two men confronted one other, because there was a confrontation in front of the gas station, I'm convinced of it. They did not part on a handshake. The big question is whether their lovers' rivalry was put into words, whether Jeanne was at the centre of the dispute or whether Jones went after my father simply because he was somewhere he shouldn't have been, accompanying communists in a police car.

— Did you fight?

I saw the stirrings of a smile on his lips.

No matter what the supposed reason for the dispute, I believe my father was the victor. Jones ordered him to get out of the car, he refused, silently or raging, I'll never know (I think he would have gone with passive resistance), and the car headed off to Ville Marie, taking Jeanne to jail and my father to another turning point in his life. Was that how it happened?

He didn't react.

It was impossible to bring up the circumstances of his first disappearance without him taking refuge behind a sort of proud sense of propriety that we could never extract anything from. He was missing for ten days, and he came back without any explanation. Ten days carefully counted by my mother, who, in spite of the anxiety, didn't panic. It wasn't her trust in God that gave her that serenity. No, she simply believed in the power of her love.

—The important thing isn't to be loved, but to love.

He granted me those few words.

Talking about grand sentiment always inspired him. We were going to talk about love. Love that comes and goes, love that stays, love that takes, and love that gives, love, supreme and commanding, which has a law all its own and which brings you to the threshold of happiness. To the threshold?

— Love isn't happiness. It's too big to fit into something so small.

I think about my mother, who found her happiness in a thimble.

— Happiness is great, but when you have love, true love …

My mother welcomed him back with open arms, without asking him where he had been or what he had done during those ten days, too happy to have him back in the bosom of the family. He, too tired or oblivious, fell into a chair and announced that from that point on he would devote himself to the people's revolution.

— Happiness is the feeling of being in one's proper place in life.

Our little apartment on Dallaire Avenue became the eye of a whirlwind of paper, because our father managed the newspaper from our kitchen, and was its sole employee and lone writer. It was a protest newspaper called *Le Prolétaire*, from the name of the Bolshevik newspaper published at the dawn of the Russian Revolution and managed by Zinoviev, Lenin's top lieutenant. My father's choice of names, whether for his daughters or his newspapers, was never an innocent one.

I wasn't yet born when *Le Prolétaire* was being published; my sisters were just babies, Alexandra only a year old and Clara just one month. My father wrote his articles surrounded by diapers drying on lines hung in the kitchen — my mother couldn't hang them outside in bad weather — and he stacked his papers all around the apartment. We lived like that, in the dust of paper and the thrill of the fight, on the little that people agreed to give for *Le Prolétaire*, and later for *L'Étincelle, L'Étoile*, and *L'Aurore*.

Vaara's envelopes started to appear at our table. Discreet, barely visible under the napkin, but bursting with notes, they were what saved us from total indigence. My mother would deftly slip the napkin and the envelope into the pocket of her apron while clearing the table. As for my father, he received his share of generosity every time the printer sent him a threatening letter.

Vaara was our protector, much to my father's chagrin, and during all my years roaming the wilds of love, he was also my confidante.

He was — and I hesitated to say it because the image was so strong and I knew it would shock my father, annoy him, cause a terrible fuss, he might even curse me, but the image was too beautiful, so I risked it. — He was your Engels.

— What?

— You know perfectly well what I mean. Marx had a benefactor while he was writing *Das Kapital*.

— Engels never betrayed the cause. He was always at his friend's side, and he finished writing *Das Kapital* himself after Marx died.

I didn't push it. He was in shock from the image. Marx and Engels, he and Vaara, all marching under the same banner. He might have felt honoured, but he was impervious to that sort of flattery. He preferred to fume some more about Vaara the turncoat's fair-weather convictions.

We had that mechanical problem. It turned out to be nothing more than an ignition coil. The wire had come loose, a small hiccup that would have cost us next to nothing if we hadn't had to pay for the tow truck. On the phone, Vaara asked me who the mechanic was and I didn't know his name, so he said to me: "Look at his hands and tell me whether he's missing two fingers on the left one: the index finger and the middle finger." It was in fact the case, so he said: "It's all right. That's Teddy. I know him." Vaara knew everyone.

He took care of everything by phone. The cost of the tow truck, the repairs, he even had his friend Teddy give us an extra twenty, "in case anything happens on the road and as long as you let me pay you back, Teddy my friend, you old dog," and I heard Vaara's laugh seep from the phone.

While the mechanic was looking at the car, my father was absorbed in reading everything the garage had to offer in the way of pamphlets and road maps. When it came to Vaara's money, he pretended not to be there. He didn't budge from the bench where he sat, and he waited until I brought him the car keys.

It was a travesty that was hard to keep up, the money we received from Vaara and that our father didn't want to see. The envelopes no longer appeared on our table after their falling out, but the money still found its way to us. For a long time, it was my sister Alexandra who took care of it. Vaara would find her in the schoolyard and give her the envelope with a message for our mother, always the same one: "If it's not enough, tell her to let me know."

After my sisters left home, Vaara gave me the envelopes. He was already the owner of several seedy hotels by then, dark, malodorous places with reputations that spilled out onto the sidewalk, a pile of bodies sleeping or vaguely awake blocking the entrance and poisoning the air. I don't know where I got the gall to go meet him at his hotel one day, rather than wait in the schoolyard. Luckily I found him at the first hotel I went to, because I never would have mustered the courage to go in to a second. He was at a table, surrounded by his court of half-drunk men and women, and when he saw me in the murky light of the lobby, he let out a sluggish cry, because he too was dulled by alcohol, "My Little One is here!"

I liked those places. I liked their warm and cavernous odour, the smell of tobacco, stale alcohol, and rancid bodies, an animal smell that enveloped me as soon as I set foot inside, along with a warm greeting, "Vaara's Little One is here!" And I would be fed a feast of chips and Coke, everything a young girl could want. Vaara had left instructions. No matter where he was, he would be told straight away of my arrival, and I would see him emerge, immense and merrily rocking his shoulders in the door of the lobby. He would pull me to an out-of-the-way table and start by asking me, "So, what's new?"

All of Vaara's hotels were frequented by the underclass and the unhinged, those who couldn't keep up, who had fallen down somewhere along the way, and who couldn't get back on their feet, more men than women. Among them were fabulous eccentrics, extraordinary free thinkers, all brimming with life, who had so many tales to tell that they endlessly renewed the wonder of the human adventure. I listened to them, enthralled, under Vaara's watchful, amused eye.

He owned several of these hotels, in Rouyn and elsewhere, losing them to fire or bankruptcy without ever finding himself ruined. On the contrary. Vaara had a way with money and a taste for risk, and he came out of these misadventures with other hotels, just as dark and smelly, that he managed in the same offhand way.

I sometimes ask myself whether that ease, that ability to bounce back, and the pleasure he took in life were not the real cause of my father's anger.

We set back out on the road, and I'm still there in my mind. The car made its usual racket of burping and coughing, which in the end was reassuring, and spring passed by us at full tilt, because my father was flooring it. He was in such a hurry to leave that he barely returned Teddy the mechanic's goodbyes.

— We have to get there before supper. Otherwise we'll have to spend the night somewhere along the way.

He wanted me to believe that it was the distance left to cover that was behind the hurry. But I knew that he was rushing to leave the place where he had been humiliated by Vaara's money.

Spring passed by us, trickling with melted snow and overflowing streams, and I was in no hurry to arrive at our destination.

On the phone, when Vaara found out where we were going, he had said, "Don't let him take you to the lumberjacks, Little One. They'll lynch you."

CHAPTER 10

I don't know where he got the idea that he could serve the people's revolution with a newspaper with a circulation of five hundred.

We kept up a romantic fantasy about it for a long time, my sisters and I, imagining our father gaunt and feverish, holding Jeanne's hands through the prison bars and making her the solemn promise to found a newspaper for the glory of the revolution. Of the three of us, Clara had the most fertile imagination, and she was the one who added a surreal detail to the scene, "and Lenin blessed them," she said, so that among us, each putting our finishing touches on the image, we achieved the most romantic representation possible of a communist marriage: Jeanne and our father, fingers intertwined through the bars of a dark, humid dungeon, pledging to devote their lives to the fight of the people, while Lenin, looking on from the beyond, blessed their union. Of course we played this scene over and over.

We never doubted that he had been at her side during the ten days of his disappearance. Where else would he have been? But I don't believe that Jeanne had given her blessing to a newspaper that had not received official approval from the Party. The Communist Party already published *L'Ouvrier canadien*, a radical paper, succeeded by the *Clarté*, less sectarian but in keeping with doctrine handed down directly from Moscow. The Party would not have consented to a publication that was beyond its control, no matter that it was communist and pure of principle. My father wasn't a member of the Communist Party, nor of any of its organizations.

Jeanne was a disciplined militant. She would never have deviated from the Party line. When she was released from prison, it was no longer the hardline "class against class," "violent struggle if necessary." Moscow had a new diktat: you had to collaborate with social democrats, progressives, former enemies. The new policy was one of outreach; it was "the policy of extending a hand," and Jeanne, upon her return to Timmins, became an ardent propagandist for the cooperative movement.

That was the beginning of what my sisters called "the pilgrimage years."

There is a certain irony in naming these family travels as such, one hundred and twenty-five miles along treacherous and muddy roads, with the sole goal of putting my father in the presence of his beloved.

My sisters have long lost their sense of family unity. They have grown into fat, imposing, heavily made-up women with perms and rings, concerned only with their domestic world;

they treat the years of our youth with a casualness I can't defend myself against.

When they used to make the pilgrimages to Timmins, they were lively, sensitive little girls, and they had eyes and ears only for Jeanne. I wasn't along on the adventure, having not yet been born, but they told me everything in detail. For a long time, I was angry with myself for being born too late to see for myself the full yet delicate lips stretch into a soft, sad, and magnificent smile.

Jeanne lived in a modest apartment above the Timmins Co-op, and that was where our little family went the first Saturday of every month. It was a ritual that they never missed, even in the worst snowstorms. My father wound chains around the tires, my mother piled wool blankets on the back seat, and they headed off in the storm, hearts as light as if they were off on a picnic. They arrived hours later having avoided the worst, without realizing how on edge they were or how their muscles were aching, so happy were they to finally knock on Jeanne's door.

"Those were years of pure happiness."

Happiness, when set on such fragile foundations, is all the more valuable, and my mother, who concocted happy days for us all our lives, knew the price. She was the one who came up with the idea for these expeditions, she was the one who believed that these regular visits to the beloved were what was needed, and she was the one who asked Vaara for a car.

"I had to. Otherwise, how would we have made the trip?"

Dear mother!

When I asked Vaara about my mother's request, he nodded his head and sighed. "How was I supposed to resist such gentle determination?"

He was not yet a hotel keeper and had not yet broken with the Party. The Vaara of those days was the Vaara of the envelopes under the napkin, and he paid for the car just as he paid the printer and all the rest, because my father had got it into his head to make revolution with a newspaper with a circulation of five hundred.

— He was a gambler.

I know.

Vaara the gambler sometimes got up very early in the morning, after a night spent in a gambling house, or didn't go to bed at all, to see my little family off as it set out on the road in weather that would make your blood run cold. "My heart was heavy thinking that I might never see them again."

The first visit was uncomfortable, because no one knew what they were doing there yet. My mother in particular was in awe. She had only ever caught a brief glimpse of Jeanne through the grimy window of a restaurant and to see her in an intimate setting, Jeanne offering them coffee, Jeanne asking about the condition of the roads, Jeanne simple and friendly like someone who lived across the hall, and particularly to see the charcoal-grey blouse, the detachable collar, and to hear the voice that gave the famous speech, all of it had made her feel dizzy, and, afraid of losing her composure, she stayed in her chair throughout the visit, taking care of Clara and Alexandra, who were just babies. My father and Jeanne discussed politics at the kitchen table.

As the visits went on, everyone found their place in this new equilibrium, and my mother knew she was right to have brought her husband to see his beloved.

"He was happy. On the trip home, he would repeat Jeanne's every word to me, as if I hadn't been there, in the next room, in the little living room, and already he was thinking of what he could say to her the next month, what he hadn't been able to word properly, and what would be the subject of a discussion that he relished in advance."

My mother had found the recipe for perpetual happiness.

A happiness that fed itself and was regenerated every month with the jubilation of a new meeting. Vaara was the only one excluded from it. "All that fuss over Jeanne's smile or a word she used: it started to bore me."

My mother came back from these visits with something to share with my father, the long discussions that they replayed together and that united them in a single love.

"I was never so happy."

I believe that those years were happy ones for Jeanne, too. The politics of extending a hand brought new freedom for militants. Moscow began to believe that a social life and a family were no longer a contradiction with revolutionary professionalism and recommended that militants integrate into their community to better infiltrate it. So Jeanne took up cross-country skiing, developed an interest in hockey, had supper with friends, and even co-owned a sewing machine, probably with the friend she skied with, the Finnish woman who had taken her under her wing.

Jeanne was popular, loved, protected by a wide network of friends that stretched from the Central Committee of the Communist Party in Toronto to the entire immigrant community of Timmins, and they had passed the word that they had to stop her from overdoing it. The diagnosis of tuberculosis had not yet been made, but her pallor, her fevered gaze, and above all, the dry, persistent cough, fooled no one except for Jeanne, who had always refused to worry about herself.

— She was an optimist; she never despaired, not even of the fate of humanity.

My father also refused to see her illness. Jeanne was a heroine, an icon: nothing could undermine such an extraordinary being.

In any event, their relationship through the pilgrimage years was well beyond such considerations. The times were both exciting and troubling. There was the victory of the Popular Front in Spain and in France, the Spanish Civil War, the Second World War, and the Party's position that had to be defended, no matter what, although that wasn't always easy to do. Moscow had made some dramatic about-faces. The German-Soviet Pact, among other initiatives, was hard to understand. Jeanne took great pains explaining the complexity of the ideological imbroglios to my father who, while not a member of the Communist Party, was no less a pacifist, anti-fascist, non-interventionist, and militarist when the Party line required it. His writing in *Le Prolétaire* is a moving testimony to this.

The long discussions they had every month ensured the ideological rectitude of *Le Prolétaire*. My father arrived with his copy, and Jeanne advised him and guided him through the ins and outs of communist thought. All the newspapers he published after this were inspired by these meetings. This is how he was able to have a solo career as a revolutionary journalist in the wilderness of Abitibi without the Party having anything to say about it.

My mother brought her mending. Jeanne's sewing machine was an object of worship during the pilgrimage years, particularly given that news on the sartorial front had become scarce, Jeanne offering up only a modest Basque beret, commented upon rather summarily by my sisters, who were never able to agree on the colour. The sewing machine, on the other hand, was described to me in great detail. It was a manual Singer that had been souped up with electricity, so that my mother didn't have to turn the hand-crank to get it going. She just had to keep her foot on the pedal and the machine would run through miles of fabric.

The machine was enshrined in the living room under a window that offered light during the day, and Jeanne quickly divined the direction of my mother's looks. Her invitation was not refused. On the next visit my mother brought her mending, and then she set about making clothes — dresses, aprons, and blouses — which she was very skilled at. She found herself visit after visit settled in at Jeanne's sewing machine, surrounded by my sisters who were growing by the minute, while at the kitchen table people were grappling with horrific wars.

"Sewing is the most satisfying thing in the world."

The slightest activity was a source of a joy that I would call metaphysical for my mother, so transported was she by the idea rather than the reality of it. Happiness for her was a moment-to-moment affair.

In fact, she was the one who led me to think that Jeanne's happiest years were spent in Timmins.

"Once a woman buys a sewing machine, she settles into happiness at home."

I never developed this domestic version of happiness. I have spent my life looking for the intangible truth of my being, mainly along the roads, and I don't believe I could be happy staying still. I also don't believe that Jeanne settled into the comfort of the petty domestic joys that were so dear to my mother. But I do believe that life was milder in Timmins, and that Jeanne found a sort of balance there between her simple nature that came from her peasant origins and the revolutionary fight, less bitter, less harsh, because it afforded a little gentleness.

Jeanne still continued a very active life. In spite of the advance of her illness, in spite of the urging of those around her, she put all of her energies to good use. It was an exciting, albeit demanding, time for militants. The Spanish Civil War, in particular, required a great deal of work, because the international brigades fighting Franco and the Spanish people, who were starving to death, both needed support. Jeanne organized lectures, fundraisers, passed the hat wherever she could and, when her days at the co-op permitted (she was responsible for procurement, inventory, and purchasing), she also took care of the Canadian Labour Defence League. I like to think that the few hours spent sewing or skiing with her Finnish friend offered her a bit of respite.

— A sewing machine?

He had forgotten.

From the moment the visits to Jeanne started, my father was exempted from descriptions of her outfits and other detailed reports, because my mother could now see everything with her own eyes, and from then on he interested himself only in Jeanne as a person, her thinking, her desires, her hopes, and her passions that lifted the world up in their endless discussions. The sewing machine and other objects of reverence were of no interest to him.

He had no memory of Jeanne's apartment either. Every question I asked him about it went unanswered. He didn't remember the layout of the rooms, the colour of the walls, or the furniture, all things that my mother described to me at great length.

What's even more astonishing is that sometimes Jeanne wasn't even there during a visit, having been called away for one of her many activities. The Finnish friend would come to let them in, and they would spend the day there, my mother at the sewing machine and my father alone at the table, silently contemplating everything he laid his eyes on. Those were his best moments, according to my mother.

He spent hours at the table. Silent, unmoving, absorbed in contemplation of the wallpaper before him, or the dust that danced in the beam of light, or the pattern of the oilskin tablecloth that he would start to slowly and lovingly caress with the palm of his hand. He would then get up and stand watch over a piece of furniture, a window, or another wall that he would consider in the same way. Going station to station, he would reach Jeanne's bedroom, and be stalled for a long time in the doorway, because he didn't dare penetrate, and he would let himself absorb all the colours, the odours, and the textures that lived in the room of his beloved. He would come back to sit at the table and return to staring into the void of the wallpaper, the light, or the tablecloth.

Sometimes during these long hours of silence at the table he would utter a word, sometimes even a complete sentence. My mother knew that he was having a conversation with the absent Jeanne, who was nonetheless attentive to every thought that crossed her husband's mind.

It was during one of these long conversations that my mother heard the words that almost turned the life of our little family upside down. He said, in a tone that left no doubt as to the depth of his thoughts: "It's decided then. I'm enlisting."

She knew immediately what he meant.

"I had to do something. I couldn't let him enlist."

She turned to Vaara. Vaara was still a communist at the time, so he could understand a comrade's desire to enlist in the International Brigades and, because of that, he knew how to find the arguments that would dissuade my father from going and getting himself killed on the Spanish battlefields.

He was dumbfounded to see her walk into the lobby of the Nickel Range Hotel. She was surprised to be there herself, standing in the middle of the lobby, the only woman in the place, surrounded by men she didn't know, drunkards who were sleeping off the night before in a chair, and she hung on to her coat, from fear or from fragility, practically clinging to it bodily. "She was touching, very moving."

Vaara doesn't regret what he did. "There wasn't a single family man among the volunteers in the International Brigades."

As for my father, he felt as though the Spanish Civil War had been stolen from him.

— I missed my only opportunity to kill a fascist with my own hands.

How could he have believed that he could do such a thing? He, so civil, of such a delicate constitution, how could he have fought hand-to-hand with an enraged fascist? How could he have stood seeing a comrade's guts spill out? How could he have come through the war unscathed, he who was all refinement, all elegance, all pardon-me-and-please? He didn't have what it takes. These aren't the arguments that Vaara used, of course. My father would never have stood for it.

"Writing is the noblest of fights," Vaara pointed out. "Marx didn't wage one war, but all the wars for liberation." And it was Vaara who went to fight in Spain while my father continued his fight in *Le Prolétaire*.

Before leaving, he did the rounds of the gambling houses, and won a hotel, his first, with a royal flush in hearts. And during his two years in Spain, a drinking buddy who was managing his hotel came to bring us our survival envelope.

CHAPTER 11

— A TURNCOAT.

I know. A gambler, a hedonist, and a turncoat, the regular salvo of insults, and if he had dared, he would have added another: a thief. Vaara was a thief. He stole the Spanish Civil War from him. He stole his only chance to be a hero, but the accusation was too childish, so he said nothing.

Vaara was, in fact, a war hero. He was in the Battle of Jarama, the Battle of Teruel, and in the final year, he was behind enemy lines, among the saboteurs, a special squad in charge of blowing up bridges, trains, and roads to slow Franco's advance. He saw his comrades' heads ripped off during a bombardment, he saw emaciated dogs throw themselves on open stomachs, he saw unimaginable horrors and yet, at no point did he fear for his life. "I was protected," he told me, making a half gesture to take out a small object from underneath his shirt, the scapular of Lenin, which he hadn't worn around his neck for a long time and which he pretended to kiss. With Vaara, it's hard to tell irony from injury.

He came through unscathed, aside from a slight limp, "a burst of affection from a shell in Caspe."

The Spanish Civil War was his Himalayas, his Everest. He had a great deal of nostalgia for the international comradeship of the Spanish battlefields, but he talked about it rarely, out of respect for my father's torment, who he continued to protect in spite of the insults. Gambler, hedonist, turncoat, he knew them all, for my father never let an opportunity go by to slip one in. The town wasn't big enough for them to avoid one other, and each meeting was difficult for them.

Russia attacked Finland a few months after Vaara returned from Spain. They were both immersed in the text of *Le Prolétaire* when the radio announced the news. Vaara was helping with the layout, and my father was doing a final proof.

"I've never seen him in such a state. He flew into a terrible rage."

My mother was used to blind rages, fits of fury against imperialist dogs, but this time the world had shifted; Vaara attacked his former allies, the Soviet brothers who had invaded his country and who he battered with his fists on the table, swearing on all the sacred names of the Party that he would destroy them all, one by one, with his bare hands.

My father tried to calm him down, but Vaara was incensed. He barely managed to avoid the giant's arms and legs as he settled accounts in our kitchen with every Soviet who had attacked Finland. When he lit into Stalin himself, "kolkhoz vermin," and defied him to "come and fight instead of hiding behind your army of disgusting rats." My father cried, "That's enough, you've gone too far." The two men looked at each other, choked with rage, paralyzed with anger.

That's how things would have remained had it not been for the thing which could not be undone.

Vaara ripped up his Party card in front of my father's eyes, and my father, not wanting to be outdone, took the month's envelope bulging with notes and tried to wring it to pieces, but he couldn't, so it was Vaara and his immense claws who, coming to the rescue of my father in his impotence, shredded the notes into little bits.

"Your father never forgave him."

Vaara's anger dissipated in alcohol. He drank nights, days, for entire weeks until his giant's body collapsed, and then he slept almost as long, so that when he woke up and saw a month's growth of beard in the mirror, he wondered whether an errant soul hadn't taken advantage of his absence to reincarnate. "Actually, I wondered whether it wasn't Marx playing a special sort of trick on me."

Vaara never holds a grudge, and the idea of a cheeky young Karl Marx coming to yank on his beard while he slept still makes him laugh. He doesn't have the least bit of acrimony, and his former comrades slap their thighs, too; they find humour in all the stories of when they were young and rebellious and life was but a dream. There has always been a table reserved for the old guard at Vaara's hotels, the old foreigners, the Fros, who speak their own private language, a delicious mumbo jumbo, a mix of slow, heavy English, every stripe of Slavic, and a bit of French mischievousness thrown in. Somehow I manage to understand it.

When I walk into one of Vaara's hotels, I go to the darkest corner of the room, and I'm sure to find my old friends. They have taken to calling me Little One as well, in spite of the age I have managed to attain with the passing years. They welcome me with a beer instead of the candy they treated me to when I was truly a little one, and we pick up the conversation as if we had seen each other the night before.

They are old now, like Vaara, and they still call each other "comrade," even though they haven't been communists for a long while. Vaara has retained his monumental stature, although he's slightly stooped and weighed down with an elephantine slowness. What's remarkable about the old man he has become is his hair, white, silky, and above all very thick: the hair of an angel settled atop a debonair old dinosaur. He keeps it long enough for his ears to be covered in little curls, and sometimes, when he tells a naughty joke or touches a nerve, I pull on one of his curls. "I only let women who unbutton their shirts for me do that," he tells me in a mocking tone, as if he were still of an age to ride bareback.

There always comes a moment when Vaara and I find ourselves alone. The old comrades will have scattered to other tables, or Vaara will have led me into the back room, a tiny place filled to the rafters with a miscellany of objects, which serves as a junk room, an office, and a private drawing room.

"So, what's new?" he'll begin. We both know why I've come. I'm in the middle of a love affair, an unhappy one, most of the time, and I've come to pour my heart out to him. Vaara has known about my love life since my teenage crushes, and it grieves him that my heart hasn't learned a thing or two. "When will you learn to love someone who loves you back?" He has a horror of tormented, unrequited love, and, alas, my parcel of pain contains only loves that are not meant to be. "Isn't your father's story enough for you?"

I don't know anything about Vaara's love life except for chaotic liaisons with ladies of the night, half prostitutes, half dancers, whom he refers to as "the lovely Fabiola," "the fabulous Anna," "the magnificent Judith," and whom he fusses over with a genuine and ostentatious tenderness. But it's obvious that none of them has stolen his heart. When it comes to feelings, it seems that we were on the receiving end of everything he had to give. Our little family was his only emotional anchor in this world, in spite of the sad story of politics that closed our door to him.

He was much more than a provider to us. He was our protector, our guardian angel, the person we turned to when things went wrong. And there was no lack of opportunity. Our father went astray so often.

My mother also got used to Vaara's hotels. When he would see her arrive, a headscarf haphazardly tied and her coat held against her, he knew that she had just extricated herself from a great deal of bother. She stopped fearing the milling bodies, the confused muttering, and the strong odour of drunks that greeted her when she walked into the lobby, and if, in a sudden fit of delirium, one of them screamed at some spectre from the past he thought he recognized in her, dear Mother Courage clutched her coat grimly to her and, with a determined step, without waiting for Vaara to come meet her, made her way through the bowels of the room to the cluttered little place where she could enter without knocking.

How I would have liked to have been a fly on the wall to hear what must have been said behind that door!

Vaara never divulged any secrets, not a single one. He didn't breathe a word, except to praise my mother's qualities, an exceptional woman, strong and courageous, and she, with the same admiring and contemplative tone, commended to my prayers the man who stopped our father from going and getting himself killed in Spain.

"Risking his own life, don't you forget it."

Risking his own life. We all knew that Vaara enlisted in the International Brigades so that our father wouldn't have to. But none of us would dare mention it, not even Alexandra, who had a ready tongue she had to bite out of fear she would blurt it out.

— Risking his own life. The things people say. At worst, he was pushing paper somewhere in a camp, and he fell off his chair and hurt his leg.

Our father never got over his anger.

When Vaara sobered up and shaved the beard left by the cheeky young ghost of Karl Marx, he came to see my father straight away to explain. "I had left the Party, permanently. I wasn't going to change my mind, but I wanted to apologize. I shouldn't have torn up the envelope."

Our door remained closed to him. Our father was on the other side of it, hand on the doorknob, white with anger, paralyzed with bitterness. He didn't bat an eye while Vaara shouted himself hoarse explaining, apologizing, and losing his temper in turn. The anger rose on either side of the door. Vaara would have let himself be blinded by a destructive rage; he would have torn everything down if my mother hadn't been looking on beseechingly behind my father. "I could only do what she wanted."

He went on another month-long bender.

I don't know how, in such a small town, two men can pretend not to see one another and continue to keep such strong feelings inside. I saw them at it so many times, on Avenue Principale, walking along the same sidewalk, and then one of them, or both of them, would abruptly change direction, or change sidewalks, or rush into a store to avoid meeting the other, to avoid catching the other's eye. Every time, I wondered which of the two was suffering more, which one had the most to lose from contact with the other, who was the first to start these complicated manoeuvres, which one of them was calling the tune.

I tend to think that my father was the one who started the pigheadedness and that Vaara kept dodging him out of respect for his feelings. It's making Vaara come off best, I know, but he has the instinct of a protector. Even though he has turned into a broken-down mammoth, I can still feel his great protective wings envelop me as soon as I set foot inside his shambles of a room.

But I don't believe that his protective instinct shielded him from his own feelings. When he talks to me about my father, his voice drops in pitch. Gesturing like a great debonair animal can't hide it: there's sadness in his voice.

He told me that there were mornings when he woke up sure that he would run into him. When your first thought of the morning presages the inevitable, how do you avoid it? "And of course, I would see him in the street, and since I had had warning we would meet, I could avoid him. I could watch him from afar to see how things were going."

I never knew whether the opposite was true, whether my father, alerted by a morning thought, lay in wait somewhere to observe Vaara without his knowing. What I do know is that there were meetings. The town was too small for two men never to be thrown together. They would sometimes cross paths in the street, find themselves alongside one another in a crowd, and each time, after the surprised looks, the insults would come, silent, angry, and still as resonant in spite of the years that had passed.

"He never forgave him."

What stung most was not the torn envelope or the break with the Party. The worst affront was being told by a gambler, a hedonist, and a turncoat that you should take care of your wife rather than chasing rainbows.

— Jeanne, a rainbow!

CHAPTER 12

JEANNE DIED ON May 7, 1944, the year of my birth.
We had several theatrical versions of this event. The most moving was the one where I was laid out on the bed, near death, but without groaning or making other inelegant noises generally attributed to the dying. Standing to my right, Clara, wearing a nurse's cap, sponged my forehead and offered consoling words. Our father, played by Alexandra, was on the other side of the bed holding Jeanne's hand.

There are inaccuracies and even downright lies in the scene, but that was how we liked to play it. We played entirely fabricated scenes, like the one in which Stalin visits Jeanne in the sanatorium, others that were more or less true, like the cemetery scene, and yet others that there was no doubt about, because they were based to the letter on Jeanne's missives. We had all of the correspondence. I still have the eighteen letters, beautifully elegant — except toward the end when her illness wore away at the loops and the upstrokes — along with those my father wrote her, close to one hundred of them.

From the first to the last, these letters are lessons in courage and optimism. When she entered the sanatorium in the fall of 1942, Jeanne's reaction was amazing: she took an interest in everything around her, as if she had arrived at a holiday resort. Her first letters described the place, the long labyrinthine corridors and the activity rooms, her room and its minimalist decor, her roommates, what she saw from her window and the slightest wrinkle in the day-to-day that made news at the sanatorium. Her letters are alive, alert, and marked by a brisk curiosity. The illness itself received the same attention. Both of her lungs were affected, she knew it and wondered whether the bacterium had not spread elsewhere. *I am dying of curiosity*, she wrote in her letter of January 6, 1943, after overhearing two doctors discussing a new treatment. It was streptomycin, which would not be perfected until 1944, too late for Jeanne.

The letters were kept in a cardboard box that my mother lined with pretty wrapping paper that she changed when it started to fade. The box was on the top shelf of the bookcase in the living room, and we each went to it in turn, sometimes my father, sometimes one of us, to pick a letter at random that we read out loud to everyone. But the real pleasure was to go off somewhere and be alone with Jeanne.

Alexandra very often "drew" the letter from December 13, 1942, because Jeanne had included a note for her. *Little Alexandra*, she wrote, *you may be surprised to hear that I am staying with you*. Alexandra was ten years old when Jeanne wrote those words to her, and they still touch her in spite of the fact that her life is poles apart from the life we knew then. The department stores have not completely lobotomized my sister, and she can still be moved by things other than coordinated bedding; the *Little Alexandra* always brought a big smile to her face. "I never thought that she would remember my name."

Jeanne explained in that letter that the sanatorium where she was living was called the Queen Alexandra. *I would have much preferred Alexandra Kollontai, but, since I'm in Orange country and they need blue blood .... Luckily, it's not Alexandra Fedorovna, friend of Rasputin and enemy of the people, God rest his soul in spite of everything. It is rather the wife of one Edward, King of England. But tell me, perhaps you know, would this Alexandra be the mother of the young king in love who abdicated the throne a few years ago?* And our father would research the matter and answer her immediately. *Dearest Jeanne, Your letter was a source of great pleasure for us....* Not a week would go by before the letter was sent off.

Jeanne was not as constant. I studied the body of letters exchanged during those two years, and I figured out that she wrote during moments of respite, between two attacks, when the illness left her in a state of *salvation*, as she said, and she took up the fight again, because she never stopped. *Hands that toil, hands that hope, hope springs eternal, you have to look on the bright side.* Our Jeanne declined as the letters went on. She was having a hard time staying on the sunny side of one hundred pounds. The fever rarely dipped below one hundred and two, but hope was still at hand, there to be willed. Our Jeanne stayed the course and, during periods of respite, she wrote to her many friends, read edifying works, and followed the battle of comrades, those of the motherland in particular, the comrades of the Red Army who were defending Stalingrad — our Jeanne never stopped being our Jeanne.

"She was a saint."

— A heroine.

I know.

The years of correspondence were punctuated by difficult moments, not so much because her illness was progressing — Jeanne brought up the subject of death only in her last letter and in a detached manner, as if she owed this final courtesy to her friends — no, the difficult moments during this time were not because of her imminent death, but because my father couldn't go to the bedside of his beloved. The Queen Alexandra Sanatorium was in London, in Southwestern Ontario, almost four hundred miles from Rouyn, which is to say light years, because it would have taken two hundred and thirty dollars to make the trip — my mother had calculated it — a sum we didn't have and that Vaara stubbornly refused to pay in spite of all of her arguments in the back room. It was a stubbornness I can't explain; Vaara's I mean, because I can well imagine dear Mother Courage making the treacherous trip through the drunks a hundred times to beg for the money.

The goodbye scene that we immortalized in our bedroom theatre is therefore fabricated. My father wasn't at her side when she took her last breath. Jeanne died with only a nameless nurse as company. The scene is too sad, so we were never able to bring it to life. Jeanne, tiny and ashen on a bed that she had practically already departed, the sheets barely swelling above her body, her face hardly distinguishable against the white pillow. There is life only in the feverish, hungry gaze, her worn-out velvety eyes following the movements of the nurse who had just entered her room. And because weakness had rendered her mute, she scratched out a note on a piece of paper for the nurse. *Stay with me for five more minutes*, she asked. The most horrible thing to imagine, and we did well not to give voice to such unspeakable pain, the most horrible thing to imagine was that Jeanne, through selflessness, through compassion, hastened to die in that five minutes so as not to keep the nurse any longer.

To find a way around this unthinkable idea, we imagined scenes in which Jeanne floated above her body and was reunited with the pantheon of communist souls who had saved the world. But the levitation scenes were unworkable, so we had no other choice but to gather around Jeanne's body, my body, rigid in death in our three-person bed, while a voice offstage (Alexandra or my mother, because Clara played the nurse) described the path that Jeanne's soul took on its journey toward the great figures of history. "And Marx says to her, 'Join us, comrade Corbin.' And then Lenin stands. He has a red rose in his hand, and he's wearing a handsome military greatcoat. He approaches Jeanne and says, 'Comrade Corbin, we hail you as a great heroine of the party.' And then Zhdanov and Liebknecht and Bukharin each come in turn, a red rose in hand, and together they break into 'The Internationale.'" The most touching moments were when comrades Kollontai and Zetkin came to pay their respects. My sisters couldn't stop their voices from quavering when, in the role of their namesakes, they would lean over my remains and invite me to share in their immortality.

The cemetery scene was more sober. It had been described to us in minutest detail by our father, who was there, Vaara having finally granted the money needed for the trip. I don't know how our mother convinced him. She must have kicked herself though, because it was after Jeanne's funeral that the second disappearance occurred, longer this time, more worrisome, more agonizing than the first, since this time our father's absence was inexplicable; Jeanne could not very well have kept him for an entire month at her graveside. But if she was worried, our mother never let it show, even when he came back and announced that his life was taking yet another new direction. My father's disappearances were unfathomable.

— I didn't disappear. I was in Toronto.

— What were you doing there?

The question was pointless. He would never answer it. I could ask him about Jeanne's funeral, the people who were there, Tim Buck and the others, and I would get a detailed report: the names of the legendary figures of Canadian communism who filed past the coffin, the speeches that were made at the cemetery, the number of red roses that were laid on the tombstone, a humble square laid right on the ground, with no other identification than a number, oh nameless sorrow! But as for the rest, what he did after the burial, one month wandering the streets of Toronto, in the offices of the Communist Party, mourning the loss of his beloved, discussing with the Party bigwigs, we'll never know. My father's disappearances were silent in their despair.

He came back and life was once again turned upside down. He was no longer satisfied spreading the revolution with a newspaper with a circulation of five hundred. He had to go announce the news of a new era where the seeds of the revolution could be found, among the proletariat in the villages crushed by poverty along the roads of colonization, the land being at the time barely cleared and the country in the grips of extreme privation. Our father got it into his head to embark upon the life of an itinerant revolutionary and for that he would need a car. My mother once again waded through the receiving line of drunks, and Vaara forked over the money.

I was born into a house of mixed feelings. We were still grieving Jeanne, but there was also the joy of my father's return, and life promised to be quite peculiar now that all hopes were pinned on the road.

When they brought him the swaddled infant, my father lifted me high up in his arms and said, "This one will change the world." That's how the family legend goes. My mother has a hard time reconciling this image with her own personal iconography.

"Like Jesus on the mountain, like Lenin upright on his mausoleum, neither would be happy if they found out."

And my sisters would guffaw every time the image was recreated in our childhood play, "This one will change the world," and they would hum, "The child, the child, sleeping in the night, she will bring us goodness and light." My sisters weren't jealous, or mocking. They were relieved of the hopes that our father had put in me, which turned his attention from them, leaving them to their frivolous games and me to learn about communist doctrine the hard way beginning when I was old enough to read.

I was thus born with a mission, and I grew up with the feeling that I carried within me a soul greater than my own. All my life, I have felt haunted by a presence that has demanded that I reach beyond the bounds of possibility. An absolute desire, an infinite quest that kept me wandering the roads, that threw me into the arms of those young men with their easy gait and their lionesque hair who didn't want me, a quest that made me believe that love was for me, sacred love, the kind of love that opens the doors to an exhilarating, jubilant pain I use to make my honey. Vaara couldn't bear to watch me cry anymore. "If you keep on getting your heart broken you'll have no tears left, Little One." It feels like I've lived my entire life taut as a bow aiming at a nameless, faceless desire.

My sisters escaped this inner drive, probably because they were two and they were the same age. They tacked their way between sacred love and the dream of a life on the kolkhoz to create charming stories where the women were beautiful and the men seductive and together they made pretty little babies in houses that looked like Stalin's dacha. They jumbled everything together. From our little plays, they remembered only a soft romanticism that they sought early on in their passing love affairs with the neighbourhood boys. Ukrainians, most of them. The neighbourhood was teeming with them, like us, raised in the Catholic religion and the communist faith, and they were barred from our house after a first meeting with my father.

—Young turncoats, Vaaras in the making.

The times were hard for my father. The comrades who came to talk about a new era at our kitchen table were dwindling.

The postwar era was a prosperous one in our little town. They needed strong arms and fresh lungs in the mines, and they went to get them in Europe, in the refugee camps, where the survivors of the war were languishing. They arrived by the wagonload, with women, children, job contracts, and the firm intention of burying horror at the bottom of a mine. Poles, Slovaks, Russians, Hungarians, but they couldn't be my father's friends. They radiated fear. They had known Hitler and Stalin, and they were afraid of even the shadow of a political idea.

The new arrivals contaminated the old ones, and all that was left were a scant few comrades.

But my father continued his fight. Practically the sole survivor in a town that had once been red, he set out in the morning with his piles of newspapers and went to places prosperity hadn't yet found, all the lost villages along the road that hadn't yet received word of a new era.

"He went into decline. He was losing his soul on the road."

He was beginning to sour, growing increasingly bitter. My mother preferred to see it as a wearing away of the soul, but clearly the disillusionment was starting to take its toll. The poverty along the road was not what he had expected. They were poor, desperately poor, but they hoped for prosperity, not a dishevelled old sap standing on a soap box, fist in the air, trotting out a string of complicated sentences. His piles of newspapers often came back untouched: nobody wanted them. His tours were exhausting, draining, depressing. And then there were the looks when he got back to town — a gently cocked eyebrow, a barely hidden smile — that confirmed to him that he had become a curiosity of bygone days, a harmless crank now that there was nothing left to fear from communism. And there were the former comrades who had strayed and who he would meet at the door of a local shop they owned or among the gasbags of the chic Café Albert. He was virtually alone holding the reins of a dream that wouldn't lift off.

"He missed Jeanne."

Then the stories of the glory days began, led by my mother one evening when my father came back particularly depressed from one of his thankless tours, and life took a turn for the better.

My memories are hazy. I was three or four. But my sister Alexandra clearly remembers that morose supper when we all ate in silence. The day had been trying. He had gone to one of those villages worn away by solitude that bordered the train tracks, and he was showered with insults and rotten eggs. He came back with a bruise under his eye, because a rock had slipped in among the garbage being thrown in his face, and our mother immediately bustled about him to bandage him, console him, pamper him. But at that very moment there were two young suitors of my sisters in the living room, barely pubescent, just getting their pimples, blushing at the slightest glance, and to their great misfortune, at the end of such a gloomy day, sons of former comrades.

All the frustrations, humiliations, and disappointments accumulated along the road rose up together and sprang like a cackle of hyenas in a short, spiteful sentence. "Out, turncoat spawn!" The voice that hurled the sentence across the living room was unrecognizable. "It was a foul-tempered voice, full of contempt, and each word rang out like a damnation," Alexandra remembered.

The boys quickly slipped away, and we found ourselves alone with the ball of venom meant for them poisoning the whole apartment.

"It couldn't go on like that."

And it was our mother, the valiant, steadfast combatant, inching along, who got us out of the mire.

We ate in silence, and when the silence remained at the end of the meal when time came for dessert, which was normally accompanied by animated conversation, our mother asked an innocent question, out of the blue, but that had the desired effect; our father lifted his head, looked at each of us, and then in a voice that still sounded bitter but that was less and less so as the words carried him into his memories, he answered that Jeanne had come to Rouyn before the lumberjack strike, that she had collected more money for *The Worker* than the entire city of Ottawa had given, that that had been at the dawn of the pioneer adventure, that the town was just a village, a hole in the forest, and yet, there was hope, comrades were multiplying, that the revolution was at the town's doorstep. That night we heard our first tale of the glory days.

"Jeanne gave him back his soul."

We already had Jeanne's speech. Our nighttime prayer, our lullaby, the enchanted moment of our evenings when one of us or my father softly recited a line from the speech, immediately followed by another in the same tone, and yet another, the lines wandering freely from the living room to the kitchen and from the kitchen to the living room, sometimes in two voices, sometimes in three, until the very end of the speech was given in unison, and we found ourselves gathered in the same room, emphatically chanting the last line.

I was too young to know the whole speech, and I remember joy mixed with worry when I attempted a fragmented or muddled sentence. But my tender age meant that I still got to enjoy the lullaby, my father's long hands around my nightdress, the soft singsong of his voice in my ear, and Jeanne's words carrying me off into the night.

So we already had the famous speech and, from a single question my mother asked at the end of a gloomy meal, we also had the tales of the glory days. Her genius is an endless source of wonder to me. Because I don't doubt for a single instant that she knew her question would bring a thick stream of images to the surface that would be balm to her husband's wounds. Jeanne on the road, Jeanne at the Ukrainian Labour Temple, the lumberjack strike, the Fros strike, Turnbull, and the abominable Jones. Images that reminded him of a time when he had found hope.

The stories of the glory days started that night and never stopped.

My father still came home at times bruised after a tour, but his soul remained intact. The glorious stories painstakingly kept up at home accompanied him on the road and shielded him from bitterness and disillusion.

"Jeanne was watching over his soul."

I don't know exactly when our bedroom theatre began. My first memory is hazy. It was a rainy afternoon, the torrent had not let up all day, beating down on the window of our room. It was probably the end of August. The summer holidays were drawing to a close, and my sisters and I were bored. We had exhausted all of our games and to while away the time, one of my sisters, Clara, I believe, started the first line of Jeanne's speech. Alexandra answered her, Clara continued, back and forth until the moment when I felt I had to chime in, clumsily of course, because my knowledge of the speech had not improved, and that's when, out of boredom on that rainy late afternoon, my sisters decided to teach me Jeanne's speech word for word, and they put me on the big bed, under the photo of Lenin.

It was fun. Both for my sisters who staged it in many different ways, and for the little person that I was, captivated by the renown of the great Jeanne Corbin, and we continued our theatre in the privacy of our bedroom until the random chance of family life, laundry to put away or the floor under the bed to be swept, brought us a spectator, our mother, who sat down in the centre of our audience and remained glued to her chair.

There were grand moments, the most memorable and disturbing of which was when our father burst in to the room during our great classic, Jeanne's speech at the Ukrainian Labour Temple. It was the most beautiful piece in our repertoire, and the one we had played most often. The scenes followed in succession and each of us found our moment of grace. For me, it was the impact of love, the heart giving way.

For my mother, it was the two French farmers awaiting her in far-off Alberta, whom she greeted each time with a nod of her head and the same tender contemplation.

Our father arrived just as I was saying, *We will oppose the servants of imperialism with a picket line that is as hard as rock*. He immediately recognized the line that comes before the part of the speech in which Jeanne tries to convince all the lumberjacks to join the picket line. It was the point at which Alexandra was in the closet, changing her costume, and when she came out in our father's old overcoat, he smiled, as the game became clear to him. He knew what we were doing, and he slipped into our play as if we had been expecting him from the beginning.

That day, rather than Alexandra tangled up in a coat that was too big for her, we had a handsome, elegant man playing himself, and I felt the shock of falling madly in love with my father when I saw him walking slowly up to me, with a beatific smile, and, against our expectations, hold out his hand to help me climb down from the bed.

— I did not fall into a swoon.

CHAPTER 13

I'm always on the road. I haven't left the asphalt since my father took him with me on his travels. I'm not the militant journalist that he was. Times aren't what they were. You can't just wrap up in a few sentences what people no longer want to hear. Heaven-on-earth isn't won through the righteous battle of the oppressed, but through a well-appointed home. My sisters understood that a long time ago.

I never managed to build a life of domestic happiness. I had children and was even married. I did what I was supposed to do. I coddled and pampered my kids. I loved and adored the man who for a time was my husband. I especially had lovers who kept me on a razor's edge. It was the road that brought them to me.

This life is mine. It's the only one I have. I have lived it with a fullness of feeling that only I know and, as Vaara says, what counts in life is the feeling you put into it.

I was just thirteen when my father took me along with him on the road. I've kept a taste for movement, the need to be everywhere and nowhere at the same time, and the pleasure of going from one discovery to the next. I've known the region like the back of my hand for a long time now, but it always holds out a surprise or two. A house that wasn't there the last time I came through and that greets me with its fresh stylishness, a lake dreamlike in the morning fog, a moose, a bear, or some other creature from the woods lost in my headlights: there's always something to keep me awake, something new, a detail that escaped me, and that catches up with me as I detour through a town or a village.

You might think I'm going round in circles, straining my senses, when I have the fragments of a story right in front of me that just need to be pieced together, retold over and over again. Look, a new veranda on that house that I thought was abandoned. New owners, I suppose, with young children, because there's a tricycle and a sandbox. People of modest means with an eye for style and for space, the red grain of the veranda picked up in the perennials in the flower beds, and, farther on, a hint of the same red in a fence leading to a building that looks like a mushroom and that could be a root cellar. People who lead a simple life of toil and who have decided to find happiness in it.

It's the job that does this, I think. Stories, stories, I tell all sorts of stories in all sorts of voices. I write stories for medical journals, for women's magazines, for heaps of specialized publications, and for the mainstream press when there is a local disaster, or an election, and they don't have a journalist on-site. I am my own travelling news agency with a computer, cellphone, and files that follow me everywhere, piled on the backseat and in the trunk of the car, along with everything I need for a few nights' stay in a hotel.

A while ago a communist newspaper assigned a story to me. It was to cover a strike that had been dragging on for over a year at a pulp-and-paper mill. It was a difficult experience. I couldn't quite manage to write the article I wanted. My contact at the paper, Sébastien, a young man going by the voice on the phone, whose exact duties I never did find out, was never satisfied with what I sent him. "More muscle, more nerve," he said. "This strike isn't going to be won with vague approximations." I realized, unfortunately, that all those years of writing for the bourgeois press had taught me to do my work in the subtext. That's where you can detect what I loathe and abhor, and that's where my sympathies for the strikers at the pulp-and-paper mill could be found.

But sermonizing Sébastien couldn't have cared less about the subtext. He wanted proper finger-pointing, righteous indignation, airtight accusations, and I was heavy-hearted that I couldn't give him the story he wanted.

I confided in Vaara about it, who advised me to leave it be. "For what they're paying you, at any rate." So that's what I did. But my conscience and I aren't quite square yet. I'm angry with myself for not taking the opportunity that was handed to me to say straight out what I think.

— Subtext is meaningless.

My father. His golden, velvety voice. My conscience.

He never left me.

How can I forget that he is there, behind me, around me, in the back seat, in front, everywhere, deep inside me?

—And what would you have done in my place?

—I would have written the article my convictions demanded. You can never go wrong when you listen to your conscience.

Obviously.

He would have written the airtight article asked of him without flinching. Nothing to it. All of his newspapers were written in a rough and ready way, with that combative and masterful tone that would have made young Sébastien coo with pleasure. I cooed myself when he gave me his articles to read. They would be fresh off his Remington, and he would ask my opinion. I couldn't have made him change a single letter, I'm sure of it, he was so certain he was right. Every sentence, every word sounded like a horn on a battlefield. I read what he wrote out loud, and he would wait, pencil in hand, until I ran out of breath or stumbled on a sentence, to come over and insert a comma or a period. Punctuation was the only thing that worried him.

I became his assistant, his companion on the road, his second soul.

And that's where I lost him, on the road, near the Bartouille River, at the point where it makes a lazy loop in the sand of an esker and where a travellers' rest area recently opened.

— For heaven's sake, don't go back there.

The place really hadn't changed much. An area had been cleared, but the birches we picnicked under were still there. The river swept along masses of ice in a channel of water that created a trough in its middle. It was spring, the sun was setting in a stunning red glow on a horizon notched with pines. The day's end, which had been dark and damp, heralded a radiant tomorrow.

— For heaven's sake …

The third disappearance — the final one, the total eclipse from which he never returned — happened at the end of that spring day. He took a walk in the sand along the shore, and I never saw him again. I never got used to his absence. Sometimes I tell myself that I will see him emerge from the forest, in one of my stories, at the road's end, like a moose, a drifter, or, even better, what I like best to imagine, like a hermit in the woods, who, after long years of solitude, decides to return to the world and flags me down. I always stop. When I see a man looking shabby at the side of the road, I stop right away. It doesn't matter whether or not the man has waved me down, I brake and I invite him to get in. But the man is never old enough or dishevelled enough to have lived among the wolves for forty years.

My father disappeared on April 19, 1961. He disappeared, as I explained to my mother, to Vaara, to my sisters, to the police, to anyone who asked. We had picnicked under the birch, it was looking like the evening would be fine, and he wanted to walk along the river, while I gathered the remnants of our sandwiches. I never saw him again.

They organized a search of the surrounding forest, they dragged the river. He was never found, dead or alive, and he was declared disappeared.

Disappeared. It's the word we chose. Our father isn't dead. He didn't drown in the Bartouille River. He didn't commit suicide. No, our father isn't dead: he disappeared. We never stopped believing he was alive, and although we awaited his return for a long time, we never had to suffer the throes of grief. Our mother kept a vigil. She rejected black veils, torrents of tears, the cope of pain, and she waited for his return.

"He's happy somewhere."

There are interstellar spaces where our mother stashed her troubles and my father is there, definitely happy, because happiness reigns where she has given him refuge.

I, too, had a husband who disappeared giving no further sign of life, but I didn't create another existence for him that I could hope to see him emerge from. My loves have been devastating; they've shown no mercy and each one left me utterly bereft. Vaara's the one who always comes to find me in the depths of my misery.

The husband had deep blue eyes and hands that packed a punch. He was a "felquiste," a member of the Front de Libération du Québec, or at least that's what he claimed, and I believed him. That's how much I wanted to be swept away by the big wave. *Amour* rhymes with *toujours*. I was like a thirsty animal following the long-haired boys who strutted our streets, and they slept with me if they had nothing better to take to their bed. The town was turned on its head in the 1970s. Sex was left-wing, the left drank quarts of beer, revolution awaited us in every bar, and after Montreal came close to revolution, after Red October, a few renegades from the Montreal Left slipped in among my beautiful cowboys to wait until things cooled down. That's how I found a tall, blue-eyed blond who made me moan in pleasure and pain.

We were together long enough to have two girls, and he wandered off somewhere in the night on his way to get cigarettes. I never saw him again. "At worst, he's in prison," Vaara said to me, "at best, someone's killed him. Your misfit is a crook, Little One, not an idealist, and even less a revolutionary." He never liked any of my men.

The wife of the felquiste became a little disillusioned, lost a few pounds, and went off in search of a man who would make her feel giddy in love again.

I like them tall, with long legs, a glint of ice in their eyes. And while gone are the days when they could wear their hair down to their shoulders, I like them to leave it casually floating around them and then brush it back with a noble gesture. I loved a tall drink of water who wandered around with two tunes from the radio and who then made a career of bawdy music. I loved a man who was so lost in thought that I had to keep reminding him of my name. I loved a man who couldn't tell north from south and who kept going round in circles, another who gave me his dog, a chihuahua that you could hold in the palm of your hand. I loved a man who wasn't even five-foot-six, I was so in love with love, the smell of the sheets, his hot breath on my neck, early mornings, all the things that made me cry myself dry, and that drove Vaara to despair.

Love, always love. I'm at the threshold of old age and still looking for it. "You're not looking where it can be found." Vaara would like to see me fall into the arms of a little notary who has been courting me discretely for a number of years as I pretend not to notice. I call him Notarius. Notarius has downy hair in the shape of a crown, basset-hound eyes, inexpressive hands that are always flaccid, and he isn't the regulation six foot. His name is Jean-Louis. Not exactly an arrow through the heart.

"Still waters run deep." Vaara won't give up. Ever since the handsome Andrew I mourned at seventeen, I have never stopped confiding my loves to him and he, ever turned off by a love that cannot be, has never stopped offering me happiness that is more attainable. "Love is closer than you think." I sometimes tell myself that one day I'll have to go see the little notary.

But I never mourned a man like I mourned my father. I cried the whole night in the car, I cried through my walk to find a village, I cried through the return trip in the police car, and I was still crying when Vaara arrived at the Bartouille River.

The sky cried with me. Torrential rain started to fall in spite of the magnificent sunset the evening before, a heavy, grey rain that forced me to take shelter in the car and that didn't let up all night, a rain fine and soft at dawn, a rain that washed away the footprints that could have led to my father.

I told Vaara what I had told the police. The picnic, the glow of the setting sun on the horizon, how he walked along the shore, and how I didn't see him again. Vaara let me weep through my story and when I had no tears left he asked me: "How did it go with the lumberjacks?"

Vaara always thought it was suicide, even though he never said a word about it, out of respect for our mother. I only understood just how disillusioned my father was in answering Vaara's questions.

The encounter had been a disaster. The lumberjacks were not what we had hoped for. Nor was the camp. It was a huge complex with buildings set in a crescent for dormitories, the cafeteria, the administrative offices, the mechanical workshops, and, at the end of a long cement yard, the sawmill, and the dry kiln. I still have a vivid recollection of our arrival at the centre of the cement yard and our disappointment. This was not a place where the proletariat was wallowing in misery under the boot of capitalists. You just had to take one look at the lumberjacks. Kings. Kings without a care in the world, strolling to dinner. They had seen us arrive in the centre of the yard just when they were looking for a little fun.

The lumberjacks of the sixties were the kings of the forest, and my father approached them as if they were lowly bums.

Gone are the days when workers have to bleed themselves dry to fill the tables of the rich, my father announced from the modest height of his preacher's box in the centre of the yard. *New days are at hand*, and the lumberjacks applauded, laughing.

"The girl," they cried. "Make the girl dance."

I realized that the entire time their eyes had been on me. Me, with my misshapen sweater and my rubber boots, a pile of newspapers in my arms (*L'Étincelle? L'Étoile? L'Aurore?*), the graceless girl being asked to gyrate on a makeshift platform like a go-go dancer at one of Vaara's hotels.

I smiled. Like a simpleton no doubt. My communicant smile, it's the only one I had, and they immediately saw that I wasn't a go-go dancer.

My father didn't see what I saw, and, with a flourish, he introduced me to the crowd that was asking for me. "My daughter, my companion, my life." I don't know what he was thinking.

The crowd rose up in a clamour of outrage, an anger that sent dark looks and raised fists in our direction.

"You old lech! You've come to sell us your own daughter! You scumbag …!"

I reacted the only way I could. I grabbed my father by the arm and quickly dragged him to the car. We took off like desperados.

The Bartouille River is around six miles south of the forest complex. We drove in silence. This hadn't been our first humiliation; we had dusted off many indignities while on the road, but militant thinking had always managed to comfort us, and I believed that a conversation in the glow of the setting sun would make us forget this latest affront. I was the one who suggested the picnic.

— Forgive me.

"You couldn't have known." Vaara did everything he could to make me feel better, but nothing worked. The guilt still eats away at me: the guilt of not having known to stop him, of not having said what he needed to hear, of not having been the one he needed. I should have called him back when I saw him get farther along the shore. I should have joined him when I felt him go. I should have honked the horn, cried out, anything to bring him back to reality. "You couldn't have known what was going on in his head."

Vaara has been such a help to me all of these years. His clutter welcomes me with open arms every time my courage fails me. I often crossed my mother's path there, also coming to seek refuge in the great protective fold that is Vaara. It wasn't easy, but she hung on to her happiness in spite of my father's absence. The apartment on Dallaire Avenue awaited his return, his clothes were regularly washed and ironed, his journals and papers carefully put away in the cupboards: she kept up the hope in housekeeping and lovely smells from the kitchen, zip-a-dee-doo-dah, how sweet happiness is.

Little by little, Vaara's place at our table was restored. He took some time before deciding to cross the threshold, not out of fear of my father's possible return — he never believed it would happen — but out of respect for my mother, who never stopped believing. You could sort of say that they grew old together at our kitchen table, two old friends taking care of one another. Vaara became a sort of greying old dinosaur, and my mother wizened into a fossilized little thing. The illness took its toll. A rare form of Parkinson's transformed her into a statue of flesh. There wasn't a single muscle left on her face that could bear witness to the woman she once was. Everything was rigid, ossified, concrete. But in the middle of a cast of deep, wide wrinkles, her eyes shimmered like in the good old days. "You've kept your girlish eyes," Vaara would tell her. He took care of everything when she had to be put in a nursing home.

When she left the apartment, her only worry was for the cupboards that were still full of my father's things.

"You'll take care of your father's papers and journals? They have to be here when he comes back."

Hope, always. She never stopped waiting for him. She waited for him until her death. She bought a plot for the two of them at the cemetery, and when the horrible disease finally took her, it was Vaara who asked me: "Promise me that you'll bury me at your mother's side when the time comes." Vaara will keep watching over her at the very place that she will continue to search for her one true love.

Did my father drown in the Bartouille River? Did he kill himself? Or did he simply disappear into my mother's land of hope? I haven't looked for answers to these questions. I have more painful things to contemplate.

We picnicked under the birch trees, and then he walked along the shore and I never saw him again. That's what I told my mother, Vaara, my sisters, anyone who asked. I also told them about the hush in the car, but I didn't talk about our picnic, silent and gloomy in the setting sun, or about what happened between us. He was beside me on a big round rock that served as a seat, and he had not moved a muscle since I put the sandwich in his hands. Absolutely still, totally vacant, a mineral extension of the rock we were sitting on. I was worried. I had never seen him in such a state. I made a gesture toward him; I wanted to snap him out of it, start a conversation. I was convinced that it was our misadventure with the lumberjacks that had put him in this state, and I wanted to settle the matter with a good old militant conversation.

Before my gesture reached him, he turned toward me, and, in his eyes, I saw that he was completely lost.

— Jeanne …

I shuddered down to the core, his voice was so strange.

— Papa …

— Jeanne, I need you.

He leaned toward me, I felt his arm slip around my back, the beginning of an embrace. I began to understand the nature of the misunderstanding that was settling in between us.

— Papa … listen to me … I'm not big Jeanne.

He drew back.

— I'm your little Jeanne.

Our eyes melted into each other's, fused in a shared horror, and we pulled back in the same movement of disgust.

He slid off the rock and walked along the shore. Before he disappeared completely in the sun's dying embers, he turned and tried to motion to me with his hand.

— Forgive me.

CHAPTER 14

I DISCOVERED JEANNE'S smile a few years ago. The full yet delicate lips, the velvety eyes, the face of the Madonna. A historian who specializes in labour movements and the history of women took an interest in Jeanne's story and wrote a book that I discovered purely by chance, *Red Travellers: Jeanne Corbin and Her Comrades*. On its cover, from a grainy photo, Jeanne smiled a smile that I recognized immediately without ever having seen it before.

I read it like a person lost in the desert, as if I had been waiting for this water since my birth, as if this book would give me the key to the mystery of Jeanne. I read it and reread it, asking myself what could have put the author on the trail of this modest communist militant dead at thirty-eight of an illness that killed so many others. Canadian communism was marked by much more important figures: Annie Buller, Beckie Buhay, Florence Custance. What did Jeanne Corbin have that would make a university historian follow her story so closely, make people fall in love as soon as they were in her presence, make a man drag his family along in his own collapse?

The book didn't give me the answers. Andrée Lévesque, the historian's name, followed Jeanne's path. She went to Celletes, where she searched through the local archives. She visited the place where the two French farmers lived before emigrating to Canada. She went to Tofield and walked the land where the two farmers toiled. She consulted the attendance register at the school where Jeanne was a pupil. She searched everywhere Jeanne left a trail — in Edmonton, in Timmins, in Rouyn, in newspapers, in the archives of the Communist Party of Canada, the Comintern, and the Royal Canadian Mounted Police. She even managed to obtain a copy of Jeanne Corbin's file from Moscow (three pages and a photo), but our Jeanne remained a stranger to her. Nowhere does love figure in Andrée Lévesque's book, expect for the few lines where she puts the rumour to rest that Jeanne was romantically involved with a Party leader.

The historian didn't know about the love story that changed our lives, and I'm not surprised. History did not run through the ring of our stories.

I was tempted to contact her several times. I often imagined the letter that I would write her, the conversation we would have, but I always stumbled over the moment I would tell her our love story.

Little Jeanne has become cautious. I'm no longer the little girl who bellowed Jeanne's speech at the top of her lungs under Lenin's watch. I don't risk telling anyone about the bedroom theatre, the pilgrimages, the scarlet dress, or about the years of travelling as a propagandist along roads that gave me a life beyond just carrying a name that's not mine alone.